THE DEVIL'S SPECTACLES

THE DEVIL'S SPECTACLES

David Alexander

ALLISON & BUSBY

An Allison & Busby book
Published in 1990 by
W. H. Allen & Co. PLC
26 Grand Union Centre
338 Ladbroke Grove
London W10 5AH

Typeset by Avocet Robinson, Buckingham
Printed and bound in Great Britain by
Biddles Ltd, Guildford and King's Lynn

ISBN 0 85031 925 0

To Kate, for a new era – and Norman,
who slew the monster

'Northern and eastern Scotland possess a richly furnished album in stone which knows no predecessors, no close affinities. This is the art of the Picts. Its earliest form is that of a series of symbols, chiefly geometrical but partly of conventionalized animals and birds, incised with supreme art on the undressed surface of boulders. These symbols are widespread but have never been interpreted. . . . The origin of this art, like that of the pre-Celtic language of the earliest Picts, remains wholly unknown and almost beyond conjecture . . .'

(Dillon and Chadwick, 'The Celtic Realms'.)

PROLOGUE

It came up out of the loch like a great grey blimp: shiny, bloated, wobbling with fat. The high-pitched shouts of the handlers as they manoeuvred it with slings, ropes and a winch anchored to the beach echoed off the surrounding hills. There was a pause while a sheet of plastic was fetched and spread beneath it to protect it from the sharp stones as it came slowly up out of the shallows. It was about thirty feet long, blunt-ended and almost featureless and its skin was shiny and tight with patches of iridescence such as can be seen when oil spills into muddy water.

It was the second day of June and the hills around Loch Ness in the Scottish Highlands were giving up their sere winter look for the startling green of spring. The first tourists, many of them seasoned monster-watchers, were already there to gaze over the loch's mysterious waters, hoping for a glimpse of something strange, when the Japanese miniature submarine in its fourth season of search, struck pay-dirt. In previous years this team which, many people believed, was motivated more by a desire to promote sales of their miniaturised remote-controlled craft than any hope of finding a monster, had searched the Fort Augustus end of the twenty-two-mile long loch but had found nothing save seals, some very large salmon and a number of ancient partly-submerged logs of caruncalated and gothic shapes any one of which could give rise to wild surmises in imaginative minds. Now the search, in its last year, had moved down past Invermoriston towards where the loch debouches into the Ness River and the Caledonian Canal, and it had received satisfying publicity of the more whimsical kind in newspapers and magazines throughout the world as well as back home in Japan. The order book was now full.

The thing had been spotted first on a sonar pulse beam and later on the midget submarine's television cameras at four o'clock that morning. Whatever it was, it was vast and it was alive, moving very slowly on the muddy bottom of the loch below Castle Urquhart, close to the village of Drumnadrochit. A couple of divers had gone down warily to investigate and had reported that, apart from a couple of tentacle-like things at what they supposed was the front end, it was quite featureless and very slow and seemed utterly harmless. It had proved easy to get a couple of slings around it and draw it gradually towards the shore. All this took time and it was mid-morning before it began to appear above the surface and quite a crowd had gathered to see the monster emerge.

The winch chattered, the men with ropes pulled and the huge greyish bulk of the thing slid very slowly forwards on to the plastic sheet. Then things happened rather suddenly. As the front two-thirds of the blimp moved on to the almost frictionless surface of the wet plastic it shot forwards with no warning, coming right out of the water throwing the heaving men on heir backs and overwhelming the winch which, buried below its bulk, coughed a few times and stopped. For a few seconds the great swollen blister wobbled in the sunlight and then, as the tourists' cameras flashed, whirred and clicked according to their wont, a split appeared on the top of it, spread rapidly from stem to stern, widening as it went and with a sort of spluttering sigh the whole gelatinous organism fell apart and lay on the plastic sheet in glistening heaps of slime. Two figures which had been holding ropes heaved and stumbled out from under a few hundredweights of the stuff, then immediately bent over, retching. The reason for this behaviour became clear in a few seconds as, borne on a light inshore breeze, an odour reminiscent of ancient sewage filled the air and sent the camera-clicking tourists backing away, first quite slowly and then with frantic speed.

Within minutes all that was left of what had come out of Loch Ness was that smell and about half a ton of rapidly-drying protoplasm distributed in untidy heaps on the plastic sheet.

Hastily summoned from Aberdeen University while there was still something left to see, Professor Harold Morse of the Marine Biology Department was, towards the end of that day, scraping into specimen jars the last few samples he required from the various parts of the monster. Unlike the reporters, photographers and broadcast media-men who were there in large numbers the Professor seemed totally unaffected by the smell which was now the most interesting thing left of the creature. For the third time – and this time getting it right, with the Loch Monster Watch Exhibition Buildings in plain view behind him – the BBC television reporter asked his well-rehearsed question: 'Professor Morse, was this the Loch Ness Monster – and what was it, anyway?'

The biologist wiped his fingers on his apron and, after inspecting them carefully, pulled at his neat little beard in a reflective way. He spoke in the tones of North Yorkshire, matter-of-factly, down to earth. 'From the bits that are left,' he said, 'I would say it was a species of sea-slug – a gastropod mollusc for your more serious-minded listeners – not an unusual creature but seldom recorded as being of the size which this one apparently was. They have never been studied in any great detail because there is nothing about them which is particularly exciting or rewarding to analyse. They feed on all sorts of rubbish and are very simple creatures, virtually unchanged for millions of years. I suspect this one has been hanging about the septic-tank outlets of the village of Drumnadrochit. Highland septic tanks, as you may or may not know, seldom work very well and I suspect that this particular gastropod mollusc has enjoyed a very rich diet indeed for a very long time. As you know, the first recorded sighting of the "monster" in modern times was in the 1930s and it's been growing ever since.'

'D'you mean to say that the famous Monster, known

throughout the world for all these years, was nothing more than a slug, full of . . . of . . . ?'

'I couldn't have put it more succinctly myself,' said the professor.

THE SOWING

CHAPTER ONE

This place. There are places in the world where man has lived for very much longer than here: this place, bulwarked by the world's most ancient rocks, is old in geological time, new to the foot of man. In the old hot countries on the desert's edge and the timeless savannahs of Africa, Man and his proto-human ancestors lived and fought and struggled for aeons while this northern place lay under miles of ice where only the simplest bacteria could live. The sojourn of man at this tip of the British mainland has been for so short a time that he has, as yet, made little impact on its clay and granite and even his tracks are few and, in general, follow the rocky natural skeleton of the land. It is a place of rocks and sparse vegetation, battered hills, tough little trees and, above all, a place of water. For all of the year there is water everywhere, running in cascades down the hills, locked up in lochs from the size of a football pitch to impressive stretches of water thirty miles long. There are petty streams of quiet water and roaring floods and days when the water falling from above and the water beneath your feet unite in one vast steamy flux.

One would think, perhaps, that the fearsome struggle men have had to wrench heat and food out of this harsh place since the first few wanderers arrived some fifty centuries ago would have ensured that, their energies exhausted in the fight against wet, against the cold and the unyielding acid earth, there would be none left to struggle with each other. And yet it would be difficult to find in any other part of the world, a place where bloody unremitting combat and tribal war has had a more popular run. It would be hard to find a single decade since history began to be told or written in which Scotland was not at war either with an outside enemy or with herself. And these Highland straths where the little rubble houses crouched in the lee of the hills were the recruiting grounds for the military adventures and quarrels of the lordlings who ruled these sodden acres. Of late, the periods between these conflicts have stretched – but only to bring greater ruin when the repressed quarrels of the people break out; and the grey enduring pinnacle of the war memorial with its roll-call of the dead is the most conspicuous sight in most Highland villages.

In the last quarter of the twentieth century there has been a new, and in general peaceable, invasion to stir the sediment of these grey towns. For a generation or two only the rich would come here to hunt and fish and build rambling mansions which intruded very little on the society around them. But since the technological Fifties gave the common man his motor car and, since having it, he had to drive it somewhere, a new and much more radical intrusion began. Summer bed-and-breakfast places suddenly appeared, new hotels were built, old ones restored and enlarged and everywhere, for four months or so, the summer trade in food and accommodation, in transport and entertainment, has flourished and consolidated.

And of those areas which have grown fat from this flow of sightseers' money, this place of which I write has garnered its share. To the eye of God or a helicopter pilot the Inverbeg – Kincardine – Laidmore triangle appears as a softer, greener, downland glen delineated by the great thrust of the Cairngorm mountains to the south, the massif of central Ross-shire on its windward, western side and the distant straggle of the Sutherland hills to the north. On its eastern lee there is the broken coastline of the North Sea, invading deep into the land in many firths and sea-lochs. Along this coastal rim the road runs north to the end of the kingdom, skirting the edge of the sea so that at the end of an hour's hard driving you can look back across the water to where you came from and it is only a dozen miles away. There would seem to be no great pressure to change this time-consuming series of zigzags which is followed by the railway as well as the road. There are no industries, in the twentieth-century sense, in the fertile triangle and none north of it either, save an experimental nuclear fast-breeder fission reactor far to the north at Dounreay in the last mainland county of Caithness. And that, the people have been assured, is safely and discreetly supplied mainly by sea. But road engineers must build roads if they are to survive and bridge engineers build bridges whether they are needed or not. And, more powerful by far than either of these technicians, town and country planners must make plans, for if they ever cease to do so they must turn their skills to less rewarding tasks. So plan they do, whether the idea is a good or a bad one, whether it will do untold harm or untold good. Their impetus is merely a dynamic fact of civilisation and bureaucracy and there is no force to withstand them.

'I formally move, then, that we set up a committee to bring all the influence it can to promote the commercial and other interests of this community to . . . er . . . ' the proposer, a brisk-spoken hotelier called Simon Briggs, unused to rules-of-debate formalities, suddenly ran out of words like an old-fashioned wind-up gramophone. The chairman hurriedly cranked him up again by taking over the motion. ' . . . Of this community,' he said, 'in the face of the commercial decline which will result from the by-passing of it by the main north road being re-routed by the new bridge across the firth. That it, Simon?'

The chairman, as is often so with ex-service officers, was solidly competent with the pedantry, the excessive attention to minutiae which marks the true professional committee man. Former Squadron Leader Hugh Ross, now in his sixties, was a big hard-looking squarish man of that not uncommon type: a local boy who had been clever at school and had passed his exams not quite well enough to get to university but had made an instant success in the wartime Royal Air Force. He had never experienced combat but had plodded year by peacetime year from rank to rank, always up the ladders, though only a rung at a time, and never down any of the snakes. Good sense, an almost total lack of adventurousness or innovation, no disturbing sparks of brilliance and, above all, a sense of *balance* had taken him inexorably to the middle rank of his Service. And there it had left him for a number of years before turning him back into the world with a comfortable pension and a warm sense of undramatic and worthy achievement. He matched well with the little Inverbeg village hall, donated like so many others by that archetypal homecoming Scot, Andrew Carnegie, a lifetime ago, and tricked out as that puritanical entrepreneur had stipulated in severe and functional lines as grim as the rocks amid which it sat. There was no ornamental frippery on Squadron Leader Ross either but, despite his undoubted grip on the meeting, he had as he always had on such Highland occasions a disturbing feeling that the assembly had a built-in tendency to go straying in all directions at once. The chief cause of that predisposition rose lazily to his feet now.

'I wonder,' David Henderson, an incomer to the area who was well-known to everyone present, 'I wonder,' he said in his deceptively diffident manner, 'if we have sufficiently thought about the position of the Railways in all this – ?'

'Are you speaking in support of the motion or is this another topic?' the Squadron Leader interjected quickly. 'Because – '

'More in the nature of a point of information – but if you don't want to hear it . . . ?' And Henderson looked slowly and mildly around at the tiny audience who all knew each other so well that they could all have been members of the same large family. Several motioned for him to go on, and the Squadron Leader accepted the inevitable with a theatrical sigh to show his disapproval. This was not going to be a tidy meeting but he would make it as tidy as he could. They needed people like Henderson, who had much experience of the world and who seemed to have done various jobs in Africa and India and had even done some schoolteaching in the area before setting up his own little tourist-orientated business.

Henderson's point was this: it was clear that regional and national governments were wedded to the idea of building a bridge and a by-pass road around the fertile triangle of the Inverbeg-Kincardine-Laidmore area, making it immediately a backwater off the main national road network. But it could still have the loop of railway following the coastal and inland route and while that remained the community could still thrive. But *would* it remain? Henderson produced a copy of the Highland edition of the daily newspaper which served the area. 'There's a very small couple of paragraphs,' he said, 'on an inside page, in which British Rail denies having any plans to follow the new road-and-bridge route and close the rail loop serving our area . . .'

The Squadron Leader shook his grey head like a boxer trying to clear his vision after a sneak punch. 'Well, surely, that's the sort of good news we want, isn't it?' he said.

'Now that just shows the sort of thing we're up against, Hugh,' said Henderson. 'I'm sure you know that I once worked for a while as a journalist? Well, some of the distrust that gallant band of men have acquired for authority seems to have rubbed off on me. You see, Hugh, when a public utility such as British Railways begins denying that they're going to do something which they haven't been accused of yet, you can be pretty sure that that's just what they *are* going to do – '

'But surely that's *inviting* trouble?' the Squadron Leader argued. 'Drawing attention to themselves unnecessarily?'

'Nope. It's classic public relations. It's called testing the water. Not because they're going to draw back if it's too hot, but because they want to find out how much insulation they'll need when they jump in. In other words: what sort and what extent of public relations circus will they need to mount in order to bash it through over all our protests.'

'Oh come, man, that's a bit . . . baroque, isn't it?'

'Byzantine. Yes it is, Hugh. But that's what happens every time.'

So now the meeting had another, and a crucial, new factor to consider. And the more these businessmen (they represented a couple of small craft-producing enterprises, a dozen hotels and restaurants, garages, boat-hirers, shops) who all relied on the road and railway for their supplies and, for six months of the year, for their customers – the more they thought about both road and railway passing them by the more they realised that ruin was jogging their elbows and looking for a place to bide. They were already reeling from the loss of trade following a disastrous season in which the ancient 'draw' of the Loch Ness Monster had metaphorically and physically exploded. No-one had realised before how famous their monster had become, that it had been a by-word not only in English-speaking cultures but a Wonder of the World wherever men were interested in the mysterious and the unknown.

And so they talked for a long time, suggestion and counter-suggestion, sense and nonsense, calm acceptance and panic-stricken rejection. And in the end they passed a resolution. It read: 'This committee calls upon the Highland Regional Council to put in hand measures to avoid the interests of this community being damaged by the by-passing of the area by the road bridge across the firth and realignment of the main route north. It further requests a visit by representatives of the Council to hear the views of this committee and to make proposals.'

But it said nothing about the railway line, on the principle of not hollering until you are kicked. And as David Henderson remarked to his friend Simon Briggs the hotelier as they watched the good citizens of Inverbeg-Kincardine-Laidmore hurrying out of the hall to the pub: 'I don't know why we bother. That half-baked resolution of theirs has the weary smell of death on it before they've even sent it off. Did you notice it was written in pure "municipalese"?'

'What's municipalese, for Christ's sake?'

Henderson said: 'I thought everyone knew, but maybe it's an old journalists' term. It's that horrible, debased form of English spoken by Town Clerks and Aldermen; it's used to give an official gloss to jejune and foolish ideas and make them sound pompous and important.'

'Well, if you're so smart,' said Simon, 'why didn't you do something to change it?'

'I don't think there's any point. This isn't the way we're going to save the place. I mean, all these poor sods won't know what's happening to them till the arse is out of their breeks and the slates are coming off their roofs and they haven't the money to repair either.'

Simon was pinching his left ear and snuffling in an agitated way as he always did when he was nervous and upset. 'A good half of them won't know what's hit them even then,' he said.

A little later, when the two men were seated in that place where all Highland business, whether social or commercial, is conducted – a quiet corner of a public bar – they mulled over the unsatisfactory outcome of the save-the-community meeting and the origins and causes of the decline in trade. Tourism had had only a brief efflorescence of maybe a dozen years in their area, unlike the venerable resorts of Loch Lomond and Balmoral, famed in song and legend. It was a recent benefaction for most Highland areas and one increasingly welcomed in a place where agriculture, at its best, offered only a marginal return for great labour. Tourism demanded only simple requirements for the harvest it brought: spruced-up hotels, caravan and camping sites laid out on fields which from time immemorial had produced a few tough sheep or a half-ton of oats, the use of a spare room in a cottage for bed-and-breakfast visitors . . . and very little reward for the tax collectors of the Inland Revenue department. Highlanders had taken to it with great resilience and entrepreneurship. Almost overnight, Highland Traditional Crafts from macrame to ornamental wood-carving – crafts unknown in the area's entire history – had suddenly been discovered and exploited in hundreds of little craft workshops and 'gift' shops. Some of the more recherché rediscovered crafts even included the sale of bits of polished granite and the manufacture of traditional boomerangs; Henderson himself had set up a small 'traditional' tea-room and pottery, making lamps, mugs, ashtrays, pottery clocks and drinking vessels of shapes and textures no old Highlander would have recognised. In a good year this made him a decent living. Briggs' hotel had had a facelift it had needed for many years. Chalets had been put up in the hotel grounds and instead of the echoing empty corridors of yesteryear the place resounded now, in a good season, to the throb of discos and the tramp of visitors cramming his every nook and cranny.

'Trouble is,' Henderson observed over his second pint of Export ale, 'I've grown accustomed to their faces, these visitors. My expectations have risen. And so has my overdraft. I owe the bank ten times more than I did when I didn't know where the next bawbee was coming from. I *like* being an exploiting and greedy capitalist and I don't want to be poor and honest again.'

Simon never joked about money. He snuffled like a hamster in a box and pulled at his left ear until it grew quite red and swollen. 'If that road and rail link passes us by, I reckon I'm sunk,' he said. 'Those bloody Japanese! Why couldn't they leave things alone, eh? I mean, I don't know how many people really believed in a Loch Ness Monster. I mean, I didn't. But they *talked* about it. It was a legend. But to have it found and then burst all at the same time – I mean now everyone *knows* there's nothing there – '

'You could sell up,' Henderson said. 'It's a valuable property – '

'At least half of it belongs to the bank,' Simon shouted, then, realising other people could hear, continued in a fierce whisper: 'I couldn't sell my share for twopence until we know what effect the road bridge'll have. There's a rule about business. It has to grow all the time. If it stops growing it soon shrinks back to nothing. My hotel's stopped growing.'

There was a pause for much snuffling while Henderson watched him anxiously. Simon was an insecure man who needed a star to steer by. He ached for a faith or a leader to follow but, having found such a faith, could paradoxically reject it again without reason. He was a spare, energetic, volatile man subject to violently contrasting moods. Black despair at breakfast time was frequently transmuted by what Henderson thought of as some strange glandular malfunction to an equally irrational euphoria by tea-time. Simon knew very well he was a moody man and that these moods sprang usually from no rational basis, but this self-knowledge was no help. Any close intimate relationship with him was for this reason almost impossible to sustain and his wife had left to live with her aged mother these ten years, unable or unwilling any longer to endure his roller-coaster personality. She had said before she left him for the last time that she felt like the woman in the advertisement with five husbands and she never knew each morning which one she would wake up with. 'I'm a monogamist, Simon,' she said. 'Goodbye.'

Sometimes his children visited him briefly when they were in financial need. There was a rumour of a more than friendly relationship with his receptionist but she was a lady of such impenetrable dourness that nobody could be quite sure if their liaison was a romantic one or merely a non-aggression pact between them. And now Simon was showing signs of slipping over into one of his morose phases. David Henderson set about anxiously to prick him into life, for he wanted a little more commitment from him before he left him to his cares.

And so he leaned forward, trying to give urgency to his words. 'What we need to save this area from extinction, Simon, is a "draw", an attraction such as we had at Loch Ness. It doesn't even have to be anything real – the Monster was a legend, after all. People never actually saw it. Well, only once, anyway. But it could be an idea, a slogan even – '

'I don't know what you're talking about,' Simon said. 'I don't understand you. A monster . . . a slogan, what I mean is: what do you mean? You can't just invent something and people'll come. There has to *be* something. What?'

'Look, Simon. Every great tourist attraction in the world has got something unique. A great mountain. Pyramids. A cave. You know. It could be something beautiful or something horrible. Or something mysterious.' The words ran out for a moment. Simon stared at him in total incomprehension.

'Like what?' he said.

'Oh, I don't know yet. But I've got some vague notions kicking around. Nothing definite, yet. What I want you to do is think about it – anything, feasible or not, and we'll work on it. Think. Scheme. Plan. Ask around. Christ man, our livelihoods are at stake. We must come up with something – and soon.'

He finished his beer. He offered to pay but Simon uncharacteristically waved him away. He stood up and went to the door. There was only one other person in the bar and he was so drunk he had almost ceased to breathe some hours ago. He turned at the exit and stared solemnly at Simon for a moment before he went out into the night. 'Forget Squadron Leader Bloody Ross and his joke committee. He'll only widen the roads and put up No Parking signs. Think of a ploy.' And he was gone.

Simon shook his head, thought for a bit, then got up and went to his office. He couldn't imagine what David Henderson meant. All journalists were unreliable fellows, he thought, even – or perhaps more especially – retired ones. The poor chap was getting a bit fanciful, he decided. He needed a good woman to look after him. He decided to go and chat to his receptionist.

CHAPTER TWO

The art of ferreting for rabbits is an arcane and frustrating pastime. At almost no time in the year is it absolutely the right season for setting the ferret to work. In the winter, with a covering of snow on the ground, the big buck rabbits and the mature does which have survived into this season will stand their ground when that fearsome questing snout with its pinkish eyes maniacally aglow comes creeping like Satan into their cosy underground world. Rarely do the rabbits panic and run where the ferret-handler waits with his nets and bag above. And in the winter the rabbits are thin and stringy and not worth eating anyway. In the spring when the roads and hillocks and railway embankments are teeming with fortnight-old bunnies, the does are usually nursing a brood and they will refuse to leave their young, and so the ferret will kill below ground, will stay and have his fill, curl up and go to sleep leaving his handler fretting on the surface for hours before he reappears and consents to be taken home. In the summer it is, of course, impossible. There are plenty of rabbits and they will panic and run as they are supposed to, but because of the dense cover above-ground of grasses, heather and bushes it is rarely possible to find and seal with nets all the warren's bolt-holes and so the panic-stricken rabbits burst to the surface and escape.

Autumn, though, is a time when ferreting is just possible if you can find the right warren, net it circumspectly, and if you have a ferret who isn't so hungry he'll kill and eat without ceremony the first rabbit he meets down there in the nightmare dark, nor yet so fat he'll only go partway down into the warren and then come idly out again, telling you there was no-one down there. Autumn is, indeed, the only time to go ferreting with any chance of success and David Henderson and a young friend called Swacky – a Gaelic by-name implying speed and subtlety – set out that autumn to 'work' the side of a hill called Cnocdruidh, or The Wizard, above Henderson's place. Swacky was a cheerful fellow of twenty-three or so with some fairly anarchistic notions about private property, especially when that private property consisted of salmon on their spring run into the hill streams from the sea or deer when there was no fence around them to indicate which lairdling owned which stag or indeed if anyone owned any of them. He had an idiosyncratic habit of conversation, born perhaps of a certain difficulty of communication, of repeating something just said in slightly altered words as if the notion had been his own. Thus, when Henderson said: 'If we start on the far side of the hill, Swacky, and work our way towards the house we should be in the right place by lunchtime, OK?', Swacky, busily assembling his gear and checking his ferret box to make sure all was well with the ferocious little monster, gave the point long reflection. Eventually, he said: 'You know, Dave, it'll be dinner time before we're finished here. Let's start on the far side and come back to here. Less to carry, too.' David Henderson looked at him in astonishment, not for the first time, but he could see no sign of irony in Swacky's face, just an earnest desire to please, and to do it right. 'Er, OK then,' he said uncertainly.

But Swacky redeemed himself some minutes later by producing one of the remarkable malapropisms which he frequently let fall into casual conversation and which Henderson prized and collected, not in any sarcastic or derisive way, but with a true appreciation of their artless quality. Those which he prized above all others were those which were so close to the words which Swacky meant to use – a sort of inner, rather than a bullseye – that they acquired an impressionistic gloss, an access of meaning, which illuminated and enhanced the original. Thus, Swacky had said once, of an incident in which a friend had been removed by police from a public bar for drunk and disorderly behaviour: 'Och, they said he was fighting and shouting and using, you know, obscure language.' Swacky lived in a continual dread of the police and the law and, because of an earlier brush with the local constabulary, a certain distaste for the public prosecutor's office, known in Scotland as the Procurator Fiscal. This morning he was anxious, though he need not have been, about the legality of ferreting in an area in which no-one had granted specific permission – and that, in broad daylight. He had difficulty in bringing himself to believe that anything so enjoyable and possibly yielding profit at the end of it could be entirely legal. 'I'm hoping nobody clypes on us,' he said to Henderson, 'I'd hate to get hauled up in front of that new Procurator Physical; they say he's death on poachers. What're you laughing at?'

'Nothing, Swacky, nothing – except no-one's going to do us for catching rabbits, man. They poison them, gas them and give them horrible diseases. They're vermin to farmers and everyone wants rid of them.'

It was not a particularly successful morning. The ferret twice went down into the warrens and twice he 'found' and sent terrified bunnies scooting up to the surface out of the suddenly-menacing dark. And each time, by some malevolent chance, Swacky and Henderson had failed to place their little nets over a hidden bolt-hole and it was this hole which the escaping rabbits made for. On the third attempt, though, they caught three rabbits and Henderson, who was a coward at this part of the hunt, watched in horrified fascination as Swacky, routinely and without the slightest compunction, rabbit-punched the squealing and terrified animals and twisted their necks for good and certain measure. It was at the fourth warren, as they were rounding the side of Cnocdruidh towards Henderson's house, that everything went wrong. The ferret went down – he was 'working well' according to Swacky — and he didn't come up. There was a great commotion below ground, the warning thump of many rabbit feet and one unlucky bunny bolted to the surface, was ensnared in the net, punched, twisted and put in the bag.

Then silence. 'You know what the little bastard's done?' Swacky said. 'He's killed down there. He'll be eating it, the bastard, and then he'll go to sleep, the bastard, and if I want the little bastard back I'll just have to stay here until he bloody-well comes out.' Henderson had to go back to his house to make and receive a couple of telephone calls but promised to come back with something for Swacky's lunch within the hour.

'And see and bring your drain rods back with you,' ordered Swacky. 'You never know with that damned ferrets – sometimes you can poke them up the arse if you're lucky and wake them up.'

It was two hours before he got back. The telephone had rung constantly and people had been calling at his door and it was with a bad conscience that he hurried round the hill to the (no doubt) fuming Swacky. At first he thought he had mistaken the spot – but no, there was the whin bush with the birch sapling growing out of it just as he remembered, and that boulder in the shape of a snail. And there was the ferret box still empty of its tenant. But where Swacky had been, sitting rolling one of his hand-made cigarettes, was only what looked like a newish hole in the ground just big enough, perhaps, to permit a person of Swacky's slender build through. When he called there was for half a minute just an echoing nothing. And then an eerie wailing from underneath the ground, just by his feet, literally made him jump into the air and the flesh on his scalp horripilate. And then, 'Christ!' he swore in great relief when he heard Swacky's mocking laughter from below ground. 'I'll bet that made you jump, man,' Swacky's hollow voice said from the earth. 'I'll bet you thought it was the Earl of Hell himself. I've fallen into the warren – it's all hollow inside – and I canny get out. Go and fetch a rope. I'm bloody starving.'

Peering down the hole into the black depths Henderson thought he could just make out a lighter, moving blackness against the other general blackness which he guessed was about fifteen feet down and he threw the 'piece' he had made for him down to the buried man, who certainly found it, because the next time his voice came from the depths it was full of bread crumbs.

'And bring a light, too,' said the subterranean voice. 'I want to look around this place. And don't you come too near the edge, it's gey slippy.'

Henderson hurriedly drew back from the edge with his imagination making awful pictures: if he fell down, too, who would know where they had gone in order to fetch them out? Hundreds of years later, would their contorted skeletons be found, skulls agape as they died screaming their last cries for help? He hurried off down the hill once more, and when he returned with rope and torch Swacky was still in good heart, not by nature being afflicted with the sort of imagination which foresees disaster and paints in the details. When Henderson put a can of export beer down with the torch tied to one end of the rope the first thing he heard was the hiss of the ring-pull can opening before the buried man did anything else. 'Aye,' said Swacky after a minimal pause. 'Ye haven't brought another one, have ye?'

There was something weirdly incongruous about the satisfied burp which followed from the bowels of the earth as Henderson made the rope fast to a sturdy birch tree and urged his friend to the surface. And then up came Swacky, hand over hand, nothing the worse for his interment save a lot of moist peaty earth in his hair and another rent in his much-patched jeans. 'You ought to have a look for yourself,' he said, 'it's a sort of cave – quite big.'

It was, Henderson said afterwards, at this very moment that the idea dawned in his mind – the ploy he had been mulling over for many months. He saw the whole thing in great detail in one lucid moment of inspiration; one of those gifts of fortune which come only once or twice in a life and cannot be forced, can only be courted and awaited in patience and in trust and which must be seized then and there before the moment and the opportunity passes. But, apart from looking 'gey queer, like a man that's found a frog in his wellie', as Swacky afterwards described it, he didn't say a word until he had clambered down the hole. And then he shone the torch around inside it and marvelled at what he saw, for it was no collapsed rabbit warren that Swacky had found. It was a proper whinstone cave, a sort of cistern of rock like a bubble in the ancient magma of which this land was made, a dozen feet round and about fifteen feet deep with yet another partly earth-choked cave at least as large leading from it in the furthest corner. And then, with a scramble and a little cascade of earth, Swacky was down again beside him, looking around with a proprietary air. 'So what d'you think of it, then?' he said. 'Some cave, eh? Who d'you think made it?' He deferred to Henderson in all such matters, as 'an educated man', a phrase used with a curious mixture of respect for learning ameliorated by a slight mocking hint suggesting incompetence in all other practical and useful things such as mending a car engine or ploughing a field or laying a drain.

'Let's have a look at the second one,' said Henderson, who could feel a great burgeoning of excitement within him, in the full and certain knowledge that a pivotal moment had arrived. And this excitement was coupled with a feeling of great trepidation lest he, or Swacky, should fluff this chance. And they went exploring in some fear lest the ceiling should fall in on them, immuring them below ground for ever, but unable to stop themselves, like two adventuring schoolboys. The second cave turned out to be a grander and roomier version of the first, roofed in, as was the first, not by earth but by a dome of rock which rang true like a great bell when Swacky hit it with a stone. The floors of both were damp but not sodden and there must have been drainage out of them under the friable peaty earth. There were no stalactites for this was ancient igneous rock, not limestone, and indeed no marvels of any kind save the arresting fact of their being there at all and no-one knowing of them, as Swacky, who had trampled every inch of the ground around his home village both as a truant from school and in the long summers as a boy in search of marvels, could guarantee. Any boy who had known of the caves' existence would never have been able to keep their secret and would without fail have made a den down here for himself and his closest cronies. But there was no sign, in all the millennia since the great ice-sheet had withdrawn from this land, that anyone, until now, had found this small miracle among nature's many anomalies. And so they explored, they marvelled, they climbed back up the rope, they most carefully put back the lid of heather roots which for all these aeons had kept it virgo intacta, they placed several large flat stones over the top of that, and they went down to the house where Henderson had lived mostly alone since his marriage had faded away, and they opened a bottle of whisky. And now, over the second dram, sipped more slowly than the first, David Henderson swore his partner to secrecy in the most effective and solemn way he could devise.

'Swacky,' he said finally to the bemused young man, 'what I'm trying to explain is that I think I know a way we can make a lot of money out of today's bit of luck. I've been looking for something like it, without quite knowing what it was I was searching for, for months and there's something almost like magic in the way we, or rather you, stumbled on those caves today.' (Here, Swacky, who was grasping about two words in three and not making any sense at all out of what his older friend was saying, eyed the whisky bottle surreptitiously just to make sure Henderson wasn't drunk but no, not on two drams, he couldn't be.) 'Opportunity's a funny thing,' he was saying, 'it only *becomes* an opportunity if you're ready for it and know what to do with it – otherwise, it's just a routine, ordinary event. I s'pose that's why it looks like luck, like magic: it's really an entirely subjective matter which is luck to one man, routine to another . . . Sorry Swacky, I was just digress – – er, going on, in my usual way. What I'm trying to say is that when I've worked out exactly how we can use those caves of yours, I'll explain it all to you and you'll get the importance of it all right. But all you've got to do right now is keep your mouth shut about it. Don't tell a soul – not your mother or your father or your girlfriend or your mates. If you do, if you even hint about it over a dram,' (and this was Henderson's greatest fear, for Swacky's every spare moment was spent in a bar) 'I assure you most solemnly it will be absolutely worthless. But if you can keep the secret for a month or two I swear to you we can use it to set you – and me – up for the rest of our lives. You may not believe it, Swacky, but if we play it right, that cave will buy you a car and a house and as many drams as you like for the rest of your natural life

– but only if you keep your great big blathering mouth shut about it, OK? Now swear.'

And solemnly and with great deliberation, he swore Swacky to utter silence. He made him hold the Bible, which wasn't really the Bible, for after a frantic search he couldn't find one in the house, but which was really a red morocco-bound complete works of Shakespeare but which, to Swacky, looked impressively like the real thing, and to swear on his hopes of heaven and his fears of hell never, never, without David Henderson's express permission to hint by word, deed or sidelong look, of the caves' existence. And then, as the level in the bottle sank, he made him swear again. Swacky was impressed; he was as impressed as by anything in his experience so far, for he knew his friend was not a demonstrative fellow. He also thought that poor auld Henderson may have gone a wee bitty round the bend, that perhaps he had, as his fishermen friends colourfully put it, but one oar in the water. But Henderson was reasonably sure as he saw Swacky out into the night, tight but fully-conscious, that he had sealed his lips for a while at least.

At the threshold, Swacky suddenly turned back, concern in his face. 'Chrish,' he said. 'Chrish, man, Davie, d'ye ken what we've forgot? The poor bloory ferret's still down the bloory hole! Ach, I s'pose I c'n always get another – but he was a bloory good ferret thon.'

CHAPTER THREE

A letter from David Henderson to Miss Alison Grant.

Dear Alison,

Swacky and I – you remember Swacky; you were in Sixth Year and he was in Third and he was the one who used to snare rabbits on the school playing fields and one day caught the janitor's wife's pekinese? – Swacky and I, I say, found a Cave last night. The capital letter is intended; it is such a cave as you can have rarely seen and myself, never. It is about a quarter of a mile from here on the side of Cnocdruidh and at first I thought we might find something in it which would interest the likes of you – old bones, bits of pottery, an ancient hearth or two. But there was nothing in it, save, as Swacky put it, some rabbit shit. It is a virgin cave, or was, never entered before, I believe, and completely unknown to speleologists. A minor miracle in its way in such a trodden-over area . . .

What I want you to consider, Ally, is something which might get you struck off the roll of the Ancient and Honourable Order of Potsherd Seekers: to give your consideration to accepting the post of unpaid, unofficial and absolutely secret graffiti adviser to the Cnocdruidh Development Committee. In other words (and to avoid the awful facetiousness I seem to fall into whenever I write to you) I think we ought to put something into this here cave to make it a bit more interesting and I need an expert in these abstruse matters to see that we do it right. And so my thoughts turned, as they often do, to you.

I don't want to say any more about the idea in case you wisely decide to have nothing to do with it and only wish to add that whatever we do do with this cave it must seem to be authentic, must fool the experts and must be exciting enough to pull in the crowds. What say you?

Agog, I await your reply,

Love, David.

He put down his pen and his thoughts went back to when he had first known Alison Fraser as a pupil, long gone now from the little northern school where he had worked as a part-time teacher and she had been in his Art class. She had had a brilliant passage through university and thence to a disappearance for some years in gloomy corridors and cellars of various provincial museums where, in his fancy, he had seen her poring over ancient manuscripts and incunabula and bits of broken pottery, slowly burying the bright promise he had known under layer after layer of ancient dust. Then, recently, they had met again during one of her frequent visits to her northern home and the meeting had left him confused and curiously excited by the changes the years had wrought in her. People thought she had become solemn but he believed this was an assumed mantle, a protective cover, for it was impossible to believe the clumsy ebullient teenager he had known had disappeared completely.

One memory of her which would be forever fresh in his mind was of her last day at school when, to the shrinking embarrassment of an ultra-conventional headmaster, she was called to the platform six several times to receive her prizes for top honours in her classes, for she had been an outstanding scholar. The cult that year was for very short skirts and very long hair and, in addition to heading the field over everyone in scholarship, Alison had led the way in fashion, too. Her hair, waist-length and luxuriant and artfully bleached with lighter streaks, was reminiscent of the rear view of an Afghan hound and, like that rear view, almost featureless save on rare occasions when the tip of a nose, questing and pink, and a fleeting glimpse of a bright grey-green eye glittered through. It was a mystery how she managed to negotiate the platform steps at all from behind such a thicket but Henderson surmised that it was easier for her to look out of than for others to look into and she never stumbled or failed to grasp her prizes accurately at the first attempt. In that year, too, she had favoured a micro-mini skirt of such extreme shortness that at every slightest move her pants were, for some tantalisingly, for others shockingly, exposed and there was such acreage of sturdy muscular thigh visible that she seemed more ostrich than woman.

A high point in Henderson's memory and a favourite newspaper cutting in his records was the ceremonial posing, after that disastrous prize-giving ceremony, for the picture of the school dux and the other prizewinners for the local weekly newspaper. The headmaster in that season was a very short, bald, round man and his attempts to interpose his rotund little frame as concealment of his lanky star pupil were predestined to failure. He could conceal one end only at the expense of exposing the other and he did, indeed, manage to hide those outrageous thighs but, in doing so, he needs must give greater dramatic effect to the revolutionary Afghan hair looming above and behind him. And this failure, to his considerable mortification, led the front page of the little newspaper the next day.

She had been just as uninhibited in the lunging schoolgirl crush she had developed for him and used to try to tempt him by brushing against him on every possible occasion – in the school library, searching for a book, in the corridors when they met – and used to sit on the corner of his desk in her micro-mini, eyes hidden behind the curtain of her hair, offering those stupendous chorus-girl thighs to him. He had managed, somehow, to steer the delicate course of showing fatherly concern and interest in her while ignoring these advances without inflicting humiliation or making her feel ashamed. She must have thought him singularly stupid. And he had, indeed, sometimes felt the demon tug of temptation, pulling like tiny barbs in the mind, urging him to accept this generous and open-hearted offer but he believed he had to resist it, and did.

Had all this ebullience and innocence and gusto faded entirely away, he used to wonder, and been replaced by the solemn intellectualism he had been told about? He hoped not and then, when he had met her again, found it was not so. Of course she had changed during the intervening years but that spirit of rebelliousness, so strong when she was a girl, was still there under the surface and, even if she rejected this attempt to recruit her to his plan for the Cnocdruidh Caves, he knew she would not betray it.

And then by return of post he had his reply, as forthright and uncomplicated as he knew in his heart she was:

Dear Teacher,

So now you want some of your investment back, huh? They always said you were a crook and I didn't believe them. I'm coming up this weekend to save you from your folly.

Yes, I remember Swacky all right, Swacky Ross? It was him what was caught a-peeking into the girls' shower room in the games hall, so it wasn't just rabbits he was after poaching.

If you can't keep better company than this you obviously need looking after, but who's to take on such a task?

Meet the train.

Love, Ally.

And, in a postscript she gave him time and day of arrival and had underlined this information heavily in red, guessing, or more probably, remembering that attention to dates and times was not numbered among his virtues.

CHAPTER FOUR

'Thirty-odd years ago,' David Henderson was telling his tiny audience, trying to avoid the orotundity of style which seemed to take him over whenever he rose to his feet to make a little speech, 'there were two little boys playing truant from school in a little south-Spain village called Nerja, not far from Malaga. It was a very poor little village with rocky soil, stunted olive trees, a few vines and lots of goats. You can always tell how poor people are by the number of goats they have. Nerja had lots of them. There were no tourists and hardly anyone had a motor car. Travel was limited to how far a donkey could travel in half a day. It was medieval – a bit like we might become when the railway and the road passes us by, only we'll be a lot colder.

'Nerja had been sleeping, virtually unchanged, for a thousand years – but what those two naughty little boys found changed it almost overnight into the wonderful place it is today: a noisy, frantic, crowded, diesel-reeking mecca for thousands upon thousands of tourists, lodged in hotels, *hostals*, auberges and assorted bed-and-brek establishments. In short, it has grown extremely rich. Nobody, nowadays, has to do anything more difficult than cheating the tourists out of their pesetas for indifferent meals, pretend antiques, cardboard leather and stuffed donkeys with hats on. Nerja today is a very happy place and a very ugly one, sitting in its invisible smog of diesel and petrol fumes, its cash-registers crashing and tinkling, its culture entirely taken over by a polyglot crowd of bemused spendthrifts – a consummation which, I gather, we yearn for here, ourselves.

'I've invited you lot here today to tell you how we, too, can become a Nerja and, like them, grow fat and prosperous and immoral. Yes, Simon, fill up the glasses again.'

The meeting was taking place in David Henderson's tea-room/pottery, bereft, at this closed season, of customers. There was Simon Briggs, Squadron Leader Hugh Ross, Monty Dickinson (Henderson's landlord), a young woman who was a stranger to all of them, whom Henderson had introduced simply as Alison Fraser, and Swacky who, spruced-up and lively, was enjoying it all very much though he knew no more than the others what Henderson had in mind. The choice of his own home-workshop for the meeting was psychologically a good one. The niceties of etiquette ensured that he was not interrupted too harshly or critically on his own territory, and so had the floor.

'Back to our naughty schoolboys,' he said, when the glasses had been refilled. 'What they observed, as they romped in the hills above the village, was a flight of bats – '

'Bats, did you say?' the Squadron Leader interjected. 'Bats, David?' And indeed they were all looking at him a little speculatively, a nervous embarrassment beginning to invade the atmosphere.

'That's right, Hugh – bats. This is a true and well-known story I'm telling you. They observed a flight of bats disappearing into a crevice and, being adventurous and curious little boys, they followed them. They widened the small hole the bats were flitting through – and what they saw inside sent them scooting home to their mommas and poppas. What they had found was a huge underground cave which had remained undiscovered since prehistoric times. And when the men of the village came with lights to investigate they found in that cave the biggest stalactite in Europe, possibly in the world, two hundred glittering feet long. They found human bones and simple flint and bone tools of twenty thousand years ago. There were primitive paintings on the walls. Today there is a huge balcony for the public to stand on and marvel, built into the side of the largest cavern – because there were several linked together – and the tourists flock there to see the archaeological treasures and also to watch, from this balcony, performances of the ballet on the rock floor below, chamber orchestral concerts and, for all I know, the bloody fandango.'

'Hm,' Simon Briggs said in the pause which followed, with a delicate and total non-commitment. 'Good for them, Dave. Are you suggesting, then, that we should take shares in the enterprise? What I mean: are you selling real estate in Derja, or something?'

'Nerja,' Henderson said. 'Well, in a sort of a way, I am – but not in the way you're suggesting, Simon. Just let me tell you one more little story and then I'll tell you the plan.' He paused, took a sip of his beer, refused the offer of a roll-up cigarette that Swacky had just made, and went on:

'Two years ago I was on holiday in the Dordogne, South of France, in a place called Les Eyzies. It's a famous place among archaeologists and anthropologists, professional, amateur and dilettante.' The young woman, Alison Fraser, here nodded agreement. 'As Alison, here, will confirm,' said Henderson. 'I've taken an amateur's interest, myself, in early man, in common with tens of thousands of others. It's a fascinating study. It was in the Fifties that archaeologists like Sir Mortimer Wheeler suddenly discovered how interested we all are in the remote past. Amateur archaeology has become one of the most popular pursuits of the twentieth century. Books, films, radio and television documentaries are poured out every day with no sign of any diminishing of interest. It's a growth-industry and on its fringes, as there usually is in any immensely popular activity, all sorts of strange and arcane offshoots have arisen – superstitions and near-religions – which bear as much relationship to scientific archaeology as astrology does to astronomy. But even so, I was amazed by Les Eyzies.' He went on to describe how, in the limestone caves on the banks of the Dordogne River, archaeologists long ago discovered the remains of Neanderthal man and the remains of our own ancestors, Cro-

Magnon man – named after a village in the area – and his tools, weapons, bones, coprolites and drawings. You entered Les Eyzies, he said, past the smartest hotel in the place – 'the Cro Magnon Hotel, I tell you no lie.' Frenchmen have always been imaginative and energetic businessmen – you only have to visit Lourdes to see that – and in Les Eyzies and many another little town round about, ancient Man is a *business*.

'For vulgar exploitation of serious and diligent work by the world's leading archaeologists and anthropologists I do not believe anywhere on earth has its equal,' he said. 'Cafes, hotels, souvenir shops, hats and tee-shirts, hoardings, touts, guides and turnstiles, books and postcards – there is no escape. I actually stood on a flight of wooden steps, eight abreast, with a thousand others and in the space of an hour worked my way to the top of a cliff. And there, after payment of a substantial fee, I walked through a cave of indifferent stalactites and stalagmites, all illuminated, Hollywood-style, with fanciful names and pretend resemblances to man-made works – a limestone cave in the old post-glacial banks of the Dordogne River; and no-one had ever found an ancient human artifact or a painting or a bone in it.

'And further away were the famous caves of Lascaux where they did find Cro-Magnon remains and the famous paintings of aurochs and deer which everyone knows about. But you're not even allowed in the Lascaux caves to see these things because the sheer volume of visitors and the action of the carbon dioxide in their breath on the limestone of the cave walls is causing these unique paintings to deteriorate. (I sometimes wonder why century upon century of Cro-Magnon breath did not have the same effect – but no matter.)'

Anyway, he said, such was the thrust of French entrepreneurship that this – one might think – utter disaster to the tourist trade in this area had not been allowed to stand in the way and they had built an entirely new, late-twentieth-century plastic and concrete replica of the Lascaux caves nearby, with much easier access than the genuine ones, with copies of the famous paintings on the lookalike artfully-roughened walls. 'So you can pay over your francs and kid yourself you've seen the real thing.' Henderson paused for breath and sank his beer at a gulp. While Simon refilled it, he finished in a rush, fearing to lose his audience's attention.

'So if anyone still doubts the drawing power of an interesting archaeological find, I recommend a study of Lascaux and Nerja and a dozen other places, and those doubts will very soon disappear. There is absolutely nothing to beat it for packing 'em in – not circuses, not bullfights, not discos, sun-drenched beaches or topless waitresses. There is nothing comparable to a good-going archaeological find, properly exploited and vulgarised to the limit to bring in the tourists and the money.

'And we have one here, right on our doorsteps. If we want it.'

There was only a minimal pause before everyone started talking at once but finally the voice of the Squadron leader came through. Where, he wanted to know, was this archaeological find and exactly what was it? 'Why haven't we ever heard of it before?' he wanted, quite reasonably, to know.

Because, said Henderson, it wasn't *there* before. And as to what kind of archaeological find it was – well that was for them and Miss Alison Fraser to decide. And that stopped them all talking. They sat quite still for a moment, staring.

'Come, man,' jollied the Squadron Leader eventually, 'I know as much about archaeology as I do about the quantum theory but I do know this: it's either there or it isn't. It is . . . what it is . . . isn't it, dammit?'

Well, yes and no, Henderson said. There was such a thing as uncovering some valuable archaeological remains and that, he admitted, was the orthodox way of making a discovery; but there was also such a thing as *creating* an archaeological find . . . Indeed he was not at all convinced that places such as the Lascaux and Nerja caves were genuine. The caves, of course, were real just as Loch Ness was real. But everyone knew now what the Monster had turned out to be: and anyone could put anything he wanted into and on the walls of a cave. You didn't even have to be much of an artist for, despite some mawkish adulation for the artistic merit of the Lascaux aurochs, any talented Art School student could do a lot better. They were admired really because of the surprise that our ancient ancestors could paint at all, not how well they could do it. 'There's been a remarkable reluctance over the years to submit the evidence to proper scientific scrutiny such as mass spectography and carbon-dating which today can establish the age of certain substances to an irrefutable fifty years or so of its exact origin . . . '

'You mean *fake* it?' said the Squadron Leader. 'Brace up, man, that's fraud. And how would you expect to get away with it, especially if you say this carbon-dating is as accurate as you say it is? I mean they'd just love to put their instruments on it – and you'd be exposed right away, what?'

Not so, said Henderson. In fact, here was the clever bit. The very reliance which the new breed of archaeologists now placed upon the physicists and their computers could be turned against them, for clever men who should know better were often hypnotised by machines and by esoteric mathematical mysteries they did not understand. And very often the dictat of the computer would be accepted even when it flew in the face of common sense.

'A word about carbon-dating, if you'll forgive a little lecture. But for this, I'll hand over to the expert – Alison, here.'

Henderson introduced Alison Fraser as a professional academic archaeologist, not long out of university, attached to a museum in one of the bigger cities. The little audience saw before them a quiet, very competent-seeming girl of about twenty-six who certainly seemed to the amateurs around her to have her subject fluently and expertly at her fingertips. She was not particularly pretty by current fashionable standards but she was feminine enough and good-looking enough to cast a little spell of charm over the company. She went into her subject at first – and this was probably a sign of diffidence – with the well-rehearsed mien of a university lecturer. 'I'm not very used to lecturing,' she said, 'so I hope you don't mind if I read quite a lot of this.' And she produced a large notebook, put a pair of glasses on her nose and started.

Radiocarbon-dating, she said, was a method for estimating the age of an archaeological sample by measuring its radioactive properties. 'It gives a date which is absolutely independent of any traditional archaeological methods and is, therefore, particularly useful when these traditional dating systems – such as cross-linking with known and already dated artifacts – can't be used. The system was developed by an American in the 1950s, a Professor Willard Libby of the Institute of Nuclear Studies in Chicago. He got a Nobel prize for it in the 1960s.

'I'd better explain: Radiocarbon is a variety of ordinary carbon. The difference between it and normal carbon is in the number of particles in the nucleus of the atom. Now ordinary carbon has six protons and six neutrons in its nucleus and is therefore known as Carbon 12. Radiocarbon has six protons and eight neutrons and is called, normally, Carbon 14. Carbon 12 and Carbon 14 have similar chemical properties because the behaviour of atoms is determined by their number of protons, not by their number of electrons. Their physical properties are different though and this shows itself in the atomic weight of the two varieties. C14 weighs seventeen per cent more than 'ordinary' carbon and – and this is the crucial factor in carbon-dating – C14 is unstable and decays, as physicists put it, to Nitrogen 14 – seven protons and seven neutrons – by emitting one of those extra electrons. These electrons are shot out like little bullets and special equipment can detect this process. So it's possible to measure the amount of radiocarbon remaining in a sample of a *former living substance* such as wood, or bone or charcoal by counting the rate at which these electrons are discharged.'

All living material, she explained, contains a small amount of radiocarbon. It originated in the stratosphere where atoms of air were bombarded by 'cosmic rays' and fell to earth, and this radiocarbon mixed with 'ordinary' carbon and found its way into every living thing containing carbon, and always in exactly the same proportion of one radiocarbon atom to every billion – one million million – of Carbon 12 atoms. And as long as the organism was alive, the processes of its metabolism ensured that the radiocarbon fraction was constant.

'When it dies, though, it stops reacting with the environment and no longer takes in carbon of either kind. The C14 gradually decays away, being unstable, and by measuring the amount remaining, this enables us to measure exactly when it died. Half of the radiocarbon is gone after 5,600 years, for example, three-quarters after 11,200 years, seven-eights after 16,800 years, and so on. And that's how we can measure the age of human artifacts of the right composition and how we can spot fakes, such as the Piltdown Man swindle.' Alison Fraser ended with a bright smile all around. 'Is that nice and clear to everybody?'

There was a slightly-stunned pause.

'I didn't understand a word of that,' Simon Briggs said.

'Nor did I,' said the Wing Commander, 'but I was considerably impressed.'

'I understood it while she was saying it,' David Henderson said, 'but now I've forgotten it.'

'Oh dear,' Alison said. 'Do you want me to go on with the rest of it, David? The rest isn't quite so technical.'

'Go on, go on,' urged the Wing Commander. And with old-world gallantry: 'I'd rather listen to you, my dear, telling me something I can't understand than listen to Henderson here telling me things I don't want to know. Go on.'

Alison seemed a bit more relaxed when she resumed. 'This next little lecture is by way of background to the plan David' – she smiled across at Henderson – 'will tell you about afterwards. Right. First some dates. The last Ice Age began to withdraw northwards at about 12,000 B.C.: 14,000 years ago. In the extreme north, where we stand now, the ice was a mile high – higher than our present day highest mountains in Scotland. That ice sheet had covered most of northern Europe and high land further south – around the Pyrenees and the Alps, for example. It had lasted for thousands of years and no life, except perhaps for some nomadic hunters during brief inter-glacial periods, people such as modern-day Eskimos and Lapps, could have been possible. The pivotal date for human occupancy of the British Isles is about 4,000 B.C. when we find the first signs of settled farming and some flint and wooden tools and weapons, but no pottery. This is what is called the Neolithic era, or the New Stone Age. (Britain was some millennia behind the Mediterranean area, where traces of settled communities have been found, dating from about 6,000 years B.C.)

'The archaeology of this period is largely a story of primitive pottery, the first of it shaped by hand rather than on a wheel, and round-bottomed or bag-shaped, probably designed to resemble skin containers. At about 3,500 B.C. the first Megalithic tombs were built in Scotland and Ireland and already these were being decorated with the sort of motifs later found very commonly in these areas – concentric circles and semicircles and zigzags engraved in the rock. Has anyone seen such things?'

Several of her audience nodded. Simon, who seemed to be concentrating very hard, said: 'There's several of those sort of things near here. Some of my guests are always photographing them.'

'Yes. Well,' said Alison, 'here we come upon one of the great conundrums of early archaeology. One would expect, and for many years it was received wisdom, that civilisation would spread from the warmer lands of southern Europe and the Mediterranean basin to the northern outposts of Scotland and Ireland. But in fact we now know that exactly the opposite happened – how or why we do not know – but, thanks to carbon-dating we *do know*. The culture of the megalithic tombs spread from the north to the Mediterranean. Silbury Hill, for instance, which most people have heard of?' – several of her audience nodded – 'Silbury Hill, which is a vast tomb 40 metres high and 2.2 hectares in area, was built in 3,000 to 2,500 B.C. and is older than the great pyramid at Gizeh. Stonehenge and Avebury megalithic circles date from about 2,600 B.C. and Skara Brae, north of here in the Orkneys, was built in about 2,500 B.C. I just want you to remember these things when David here tells you our plan and to remember, particularly, those whorls and zigzags found on cave walls in Ireland and Scotland and England 5,500 years ago – for what purpose and with what meaning, no-one knows.'

Alison Fraser sat back and Squadron Leader Ross led a little round of applause. 'I understood that bit a lot better,' he said.

And now David Henderson asked for their indulgence a little while longer while he outlined his plan, and all the time he kept his eye on the Squadron Leader. If he could bring him around he was sure the others would be no problem, so to bring Hugh

Ross around to consent — if not connivance — was essential, for he would give a gloss of respectability and sanity to the whole madcap scheme.

Henderson had had a second look at the Squadron Leader lately. He knew that Hugh Ross was a much more complex man than his bluff public persona would suggest. He had studied him, off and on, for several years as he studied the characters of anyone who interested him and he was fairly sure that he had read him aright. In the years since his retirement from the Royal Air Force with its simplicities of discipline and purpose, its rational ends (once you accepted the supreme irrationality of war) its empirical methods and pragmatic bases, Hugh had grown increasingly contemptuous of the muddle and anarchy of civilian life. Not for him was the taking on of the usual (and slightly ridiculous) role of the retired senior serviceman: the chairmanship of committees of little importance, the opening remarks at the garden fête or the easy slot in landowning society and the reserved seat at the dinner tables of the rich, where he could be relied upon, always faultlessly polite, to keep his corner of the social gathering going with reminiscences of service life. Hugh was, withal, a man who, when attacked, liked to hit back effectively when he was sure he was in the right. There was a strong core of morality in him but it was not entirely of the conventional sort; a little of the buccaneer was there, Henderson believed, and he was putting his money on that. And he was deeply outraged, far more than the others realised, by the lies, the contemptuousness and the prevarications of the local politicians and managers of public utilities such as the roads and railway authorities. He had been made to look a gullible fool by these men who were cynically arranging the by-passing of his community and he would do a great deal to get even with them.

And so Henderson made his pitch, tailored so far as he could, with Hugh in mind and tempered to Hugh's predilections. By a stroke of providence, he said, they had been given their Lascaux cave; it lay not far away on a hill owned by his landlord, Monty Dickinson (Dickinson sat up and paid proper attention for the first time) and only two people, so far, knew of its location

– Swacky Ross and himself. (Swacky's turn to take notice, though he still had much less idea than the others what Dave was driving at.) 'Think of it this way: the cave or caves are as genuine as Loch Ness. What we will put in them will be about as genuine as the Loch Ness Monster – but with this tremendous difference: the artifacts, the tools and bones and things will be genuine and the paintings with which we'll daub the walls will be genuine too, at least as far as the materials are concerned which we will use.

'You see – and this is the point of the little lecture on carbon-dating which Alison gave to you – the paint we use will be made from materials which are 6,000 years old. That pivotal date of 4,000 B.C. which Alison told you about. The carbon in the hearth will be of this same exact era and the bones and flints and jewellery, and whatever else we care to put in it, will be, and will test out to be, of whatever era we care to choose. With Alison's help, with the help of a trained scientific archaeologist, such as she is, we can do this. There will be no possibility of disproving our "find" on a purely scientific basis: in fact the computer will bear out every claim that is made for it. And it won't even be us who will be claiming it. We will have a completely independent discoverer' – he nodded to Alison Fraser – 'and if all goes according to our devious plan her discovery will, in the highest academic traditions, be stolen from her by someone much older and more revered. But not,' he added, 'by someone nearly so pretty.' And then he had the grace to look uncomfortable at having made such a fatuous remark.

The discussion, after this, went on until the whisky was finished and the room was full of smoke, and the feelings of the guests had run the gamut from puzzlement to a mixture of excitement and alarm and had now settled down to something which resembled enthusiasm. Alison Fraser had a lot to do with this; her quiet professionalism and a surprising ironically mordant wit helping to give the faint-hearted confidence that the plot could actually work. Thus she gave a sensible matter-of-factness to the plan with her further exposition of radiocarbon-dating methods. Henderson heard her saying to Dickinson and Briggs: 'Actually, it's much more difficult to date such things as cave-paintings than I gave an impression of. Quite a lot of material is needed to do carbon-dating, but we're planning to leave a chunk of stuff deliberately large enough so they can do it.'

Then, a little later – 'There's another thing which practically guarantees our little deception will be accepted as genuine: it's an attitude in scientific circles which some of us younger ones call P.E.R., or Preferred End Result.' Preferred End Result she explained, occurred when a researcher, or a statistician, or even an accountant, decided before he collated any evidence at all what he would prefer the end result to be. He would then set out with great diligence to gather and publish only those data which would lead to the conclusion he desired in the first place. Most scientific research was done in this way and it was as true of archaeology – perhaps more true of archaeology because there were more uncertainties – as it was in physics or medicine and the social sciences. She quoted as examples of P.E.R. at work, the Piltdown Man fiasco in which, for half a century everyone wanted to believe that the bones they'd found in the gravel pit were those of the Missing Link, not those of the chimpanzees and other creatures which they so obviously were. 'Professor Arthur Evans' Knossos excavations on Crete are another. We're intending to enlist a goodly dose of P.E.R. in our archaeological "find" here.'

But why, some of them wanted to know, do *you* want to get yourself involved in this? And again the little whisper of mocking irony which the antennae of Briggs and Dickinson were too ill-tuned to detect – 'Well, a girl's got to do something to make her way in the field of archaeology and they don't seem to think women as young as I am or as inexperienced as I am can be entrusted with anything much more important than classifying a lot of Anglo-Saxon sherds. And it's a hell of a challenge, taking on the Establishment and foxing it good and proper.' And when they still looked unconvinced: 'And I want to do it for you, and for David, and for a part of the world I love. It's been going down hill too long.'

Later, though, when the others had all gone and they were fixing up a meal in the kitchen, David Henderson said to her: 'You know, I'm still not sure myself why you're doing this,

Ally. I think they must have annoyed you quite badly. But I promise you're going to make those professors, or whoever they are, look awful silly.'

She gave him a little squeeze which did his old romantic heart a lot of good and then kissed him very chastely on the cheek, which redressed the balance, and said: 'We'll do that, boy, and we'll make a lot of money, too.'

Later still, when she was in bed in another part of the old house and he was lying awake smoking and thinking, he tried to analyse the feeling between them. He was sixteen . . . seventeen years older than Alison and there were times when he felt older than that. Was something happening between them? There were times when he thought so, others when he mocked himself for being an idiot. When she had got off the train at the tiny station they had stood and looked at each other for a long minute. He had said, as he had planned to do: 'Look, Ally, don't let all that old silly schoolmaster/gushing favourite pupil stuff make us awkward with each other. It was so long ago and it didn't mean anything. There, I've said it. I've been meaning to say it every time we met.'

She had looked a bit startled, a little discomfited for a fraction of time. Then she hugged him briefly.

'Didn't it?' she said. 'Was it? Was I? You never said I was your favourite, you know.'

She skipped to the car like the schoolgirl he'd known and when she was in it, like a poised self-possessed young woman, she ordered him to drive her to his home. He didn't have the faintest idea where he stood.

He put out his cigarette and went to sleep.

And now the hard work began: for Alison, for Swacky and for David Henderson who, in addition to giving what help he could in devising the overall plan for the caves and recruiting talent for some aspects of the work and arranging transport, concealment and storage, also had to maintain a continuing liaison and propaganda campaign among those in the know. He thought several times during these stages that if he had been able to visualise how much work would be involved in what had seemed in imagination to be such a simple task, he would have abandoned the idea at birth. Among the hardest of these tasks was that of keeping the rest of the team on the simmer. The Squadron Leader still would not commit himself wholeheartedly but was coming around by slow degrees in a negative way to turning a blind eye to the fakery involved, provided he was not personally concerned in it. Gradually, though, as progress was made, he showed signs of increasing interest and acceptance as he began to appreciate the sheer fun of it and Henderson knew that at last he had left first base when, over pre-dinner drinks at the old man's place one evening Hugh began to call the project 'japery' rather than his usual 'fakery'. It was beginning to take on a rather naughty air of adventure which called across the years of moral rectitude to something of the mischievous boy which still lurked deep in his soul.

No-one, though, had realised, except perhaps Alison, and she not fully, just how much work it was going to be and no-one at all had guessed how careful everyone had to be in such a close-knit community to keep the thing secret. They were abetted in this, however, by the very audacity and imaginativeness of the scheme and by the fact that archaeology of any sort was not a subject to which the generality of the local population had given any study. The plan, therefore, even though there might be some speculation as to what was going on, was impossible to guess at.

Research – or what Simon Briggs, who had some commercial training, called R and D – took up a lot of time and there were many long and earnest discussions between Alison, Henderson and Simon (who were the most erudite of the group) as to what, precisely, the graffiti on the walls of the caves should depict and what era of human development they should plant there. It seemed agreed among archaeologists and anthropologists that modern man, called variously Cro-Magnon, Homo Sapiens, and even Homo Sapiens Sapiens, probably ventured north on the fringes of the melting last glaciation of Northern Europe at about 10,000 B.C. Alison said: 'It's accepted that the first cave-dwellers of our sort of man moved into the warmer Mediterranean areas – little pockets of micro-climate where survival was possible – after this era. Some say they were driving out Neanderthal, a rougher but not so bright individual who was probably, despite the bad Press he's had, a much more peaceable creature than our ancestor, who was probably responsible for his extinction. Though I'll swear some of them survived and are alive and well and living in Kincardine, judging from some of the creatures I saw coming out of the Ault-Na-Guish Hotel at closing time last Saturday night!

'You must understand, though,' she said, 'that this 10,000-year date is problematical. There are no unequivocal artifacts save some debatable flints and possible arrow-heads available from Northern Europe at this time. It looks as if even Cro-Magnon was so weaponless that he simply drove prey animals over cliffs to kill them, or found them bogged down or weak or injured, rather than hunting them in any modern manner – an opportunistic rather than a planned activity.'

'You know, all this amazes me,' Henderson said. 'I thought all this was sorted out, cut and dried, fifty years ago. But it looks as if you can't even agree on names, never mind dates.'

'Well, it was much simpler fifty years ago, and every now and then a system gets fashionable which does more or less have it all cut and dried,' Alison said. 'But then someone comes along and discovers another bit of evidence and throws the whole thing back into the melting pot again. Truth is that there's so little evidence from this era that it can never be neat and certain but the academic mind is always looking for exactness and certainty, and the theorists keep on devising systems ahead of the evidence and then having to break them up again. But all this gives us a certain amount of elbow room. So, provided we don't overstep the reasonably well-known parameters in any gross fashion, we can let our imaginations run. For instance: it's easy to obtain carbon from hearths of the late neolithic period from about 7,000 B.C. onwards and even possible to get fragments of pottery from the Near East of that era.' This was the time, Alison explained in one of her little lectures, when the domestication of animals and the first signs of farming probably appeared south of Europe. It was thought, though, that such men as braved the icy climate and roaring floods which were, even then, carving out the sea-lochs of the Highlands, confined their activities to the hunt. 'Don't forget, though, that the chambered cairns of Orkney and the underground houses or "weems" on the mainland are placed some long time more recently than this, say, 4,000 to 3,500 B.C. There could have been, and probably were, cave-dwellers further back than this, but there's very little evidence of it. We're aiming for something not too unlikely, but still surprising: something to make the Establishment sit up and take notice. Everyone, you see, is looking for something which can be dated farther back than the current earliest discovery and the lucky discoverer will bend every possible rule to fit it in.'

They settled finally on a date of some 4,000 years before Christ as a possible era for some settlements to have begun – before Stonehenge and before the pyramids – but not too ancient for the find to have some credence. There were various substances of that era available, mouldering in the back rooms and cellars of museums and universities to which Alison had access. Much of the material had been classified so long ago that records were very elementary and could be abstracted in the certain knowledge that no-one would ever miss them.

'You'd be surprised to discover,' Alison said, 'I know I was, just what sheer *tonnage* of bones and flints, coprolites and hearth-debris is stacked up in cellars throughout the land. And how easy it is to get hold of it. It's not valuable, you see, and more of an embarrassing storage problem than anything else.' So they made a shopping list of what they thought they would need and Alison took a few days off and went and got it while Simon and Henderson agonised, quarrelled, made the peace and broke it again, over what they should put on the walls. It had to be something believable, something 'authentic'. It also had to be something dramatic. A man? A beast? A symbol – but a symbol of what? How big? And in what colour, and how inscribed? Everything else fell or was sustained depending upon the cunning with which this was done. Swacky sat in on some of these debates but more for the whisky and what he called the 'crack' – a Gaelic-derived word for an entertaining chat – though he did not get much entertainment from it. But it was he, finally, with his talent for neologisms, who cut the knot.

'Och,' he interjected during one of Simon's and Henderson's long droning wrangles, 'why not leave it to one of they astriologists to decide what to paint on the walls; they're the experts, aren't they?'

And so from this mixture of astrology, archaeology and astral travelling, the idea was born.

CHAPTER FIVE

For Hamish Matheson it was the most frightening experience of his life. With gun and spotlight he was making a most surreptitious patrol of Cnocdruidh Hill and the night was very dark save for intermittent patches of starlight when the clouds moving from the north-west cleared briefly from time to time and then closed in again. He dared not use his light because he was on Monty Dickinson's land and he was after Monty Dickinson's roe deer; for if the bloody laird couldn't be bothered hunting his policies then it was up to someone else to do it for him. Hamish was cursing steadily, sotto voce, for the ground was full of unexpected hazards: knots of heather roots which snagged themselves as if alive around his boots, and rock outcrops which could easily break a leg placed carelessly. Also, Hamish was not quite sober. He was not what a Highlander would have called drunk because he was still on his feet and making fair progress but he had certainly taken enough, and more, to keep out the autumn chill. He had met one or two people in the pub before he set out and had stayed longer and had drunk a little more than he had originally intended.

If this had not been so perhaps he would have been moving more circumspectly as he came around the last flank of the hill before the few lights in the village of Carron, where Henderson's house stood, came into view and, momentarily distracted by the glimmer, he failed to see or sense a drift of heather in front of him and he caught his foot, teetered wildly at the mid-point of balance, began to go, made frantic efforts to save himself and crashed face downwards on the hard earth as if felled from above. He lay for a shocked moment, breath knocked out of him, his left ear flattened to the earth, when he heard a voice from beneath.

It said: 'Christ, it's cold down here.' Quite distinct and close, as if someone only inches away had said it in his ear, quite matter-of-fact, as if it were an ordinary occurrence for disembodied voices from inside the earth to complain about the cold down there.

Hamish, in one galvanic movement, rose to his hands and knees and then saw something which frightened him worse: a sort of roseate glow filtering through the heather roots, very dim, almost beyond the range of vision but, as he said later, 'Like the red glow of Hell itself.'

He did not forget his gun or his spotlight but he forgot everything else – caution, sense and the path he should take – he just ran, falling many times, rolling a long way down the hill once, until he was at last on known ground and then, pausing only to thrust the gun into a known niche, pelted for the pub.

Swacky, who was there and shouldn't have been, told it to Alison and Henderson later. 'He had three drams, one after the other. He was all scratches and dirt, tears in his breeks and a bash on the eye that's going to be a helluva keeker tomorrow and of course when he tried to tell it everyone knew he was halluc . . . hallucy . . . seein' things and not for the first time neither. But when he said he had heard the voice of the Devil Himself coming out of Cnocdruidh Hill an' he was damned if he was ever going back there again, everyone just fell about. Man, oh man, the crack was good!'

(It was Hamish who, on one of his most famous Hogmanay drinking bouts, had established a small legend throughout a county where tales of drink-associated disasters were commonplace. He and his friend Lachie were so drunk – 'mortal' in Swacky's word – they had with difficulty, each supporting the other, made it to the open air outside the bar at closing time, where Lachie had incontinently fallen down. Hamish was, in the drunkard's way, solemnly and zealously intent to see his old friend safely home to his sullen wife and he reached down in the reeling dark and hoisted what he thought was his friend over his shoulder. And it was thus, toiling and sweating all the way, he had arrived at his friend's home at the top of the hill, complaining and berating him for not being able to hold his liquor. He knocked on the door and laid his burden down in the doorway as his friend's wife opened it. 'I've brought you your man, Mistress,' he said, 'and he was a sair weight to carry and for all the sense I got out of him he might have been a sack of oats.' And he tacked off back down the hill, leaving Lachie's wife staring in amazement at the sack of meal which Hamish had deposited at her door.)

'And that's lucky for us it was Hamish,' Henderson told Swacky, ''Cause if it had been anyone else he could have blown the whole thing sky-high.'

For these were the nights when Alison Fraser and David Henderson were closeted below ground in the caves while Swacky was supposed to be keeping watch above. It was autumn and none too warm in either environment but it had the advantage that the brief tourist season was over and there were unlikely to be many people wandering the Cnocdruidh Hill. Ascent and descent had to be made most carefully so as not to disturb the ground too much but, once below, it was thought safe enough to work by the brilliant light of a self-contained gas lamp. Alison insisted that this work had to be done most meticulously because for all the importance of the imaginative concept it was the detailed execution of it which would win or lose the day.

First a large section of the rock wall of the innermost cave had to be cleaned with great thoroughness, removing any traces, even microscopic ones, of recent earth or pollen, roots and seeds. It mattered not too much what overlaid the paintings: what was under them was crucial. On this fairly smooth surface the paint had to be laid. This was a bizarre concoction which had been mixed up in Henderson's kitchen one night by himself and Alison. It consisted of recherché ingredients which included ground up potsherds from an ancient Cornish site, charcoal from a Dordogne neolithic hearth and even the dust of some mummified remains from the Egyptian desert of an era long before the pyramids, before the chemical arts of mummification had been developed, when the tribes which lived on the banks of Mother Nile buried their dead in the sand where the heat and dryness preserved them. For some queer reason a Victorian explorer had brought back a stack of these rather uninteresting objects and a well-known city museum to which Alison had access had stored them ever since, crumbling, cobwebby and forgotten in its cellars. Mixed and ground together and put through Henderson's Moulinex mixer-blender (which, he said, with mild regret, he could never use again) the various substances made a goo which seemed of the right consistency to stick to the rock.

It was during the preparation of this substance that Henderson had made yet another re-appraisal of his younger companion. He had got into the habit of believing her to be rather a solemn girl: a bit of a blue-stocking, rather apodictic, with a tendency to place things into categories, as 'serious' or 'trivial'. Archaeology was in her 'serious' category. Yet here she was, giggling helplessly, as they mixed the paint ingredients in his ancient food processor. She said, between gasps: 'A bit of this and a bit of that – that's the way my mother used to cook: nothing measured, nothing weighed, nothing scientific but it usually worked out in the end. In goes a bit of a coprolite from a Cro-Magnon cave. Plonk in a bit of charcoal from a pre-Christian hearth. And in, for Christ's sweet sake, goes a touch of the left buttock or whatever of Amenhotep the Umpteenth – pre-dynastic, Old Kingdom – and,' she hit the liquidiser button, 'fold together gently and stir.' And as the machine blended the whole macabre mixture into a turgid blackish mass she positively whinnied with laughter, gasping for breath, so that Henderson, alarmed for her, had to put an arm around her to hold her up. And he held her there, squeaking and gasping, for quite a long time, long after all danger of asphyxiation had passed.

As to what they should do with this unprepossessing gouache, it was Swacky's happy malapropism which had shown the way. 'Astriologers' had turned Simon's and Henderson's thoughts to the stars and the current fad of the Ancient Astronaut Cult and had reminded Henderson of an old book he had read as a boy. There had been a sort of numbed silence in David Henderson's brain for many moments after Swacky had sounded that note and then, from a dozen different directions at once, tendrils of ideas of many sorts had reached, coalesced and formed a pattern in his mind. But the basis of the idea, he told Simon, was that book, published some time in the 1930s, long out of print, and entitled unimaginatively *The Riddle of Pre-Historic Britain*: not a title designed to reach out and grab the attention of a schoolboy. 'I found it on the shelves of the local library when I was looking for something quite different,' he told Simon, 'and it was already out of print, I think. This was in about 1960. But I took it home and I read it and it was such a lovely idea that I tried on and off for a couple of years to believe it, but in the end I couldn't. Even the name of the author struck one as romantic and unlikely; he was called Comyns Beaumont.' Simon had begun to get restive, so Henderson rapidly outlined the burden of Beaumont's idea. Beaumont had gathered the 'evidence' for his theory from four main sources, he said: from early myths (always a happy hunting ground for the weirder fringes of speculation), from the remarkable sculptured 'Pictish' stones of Scotland, from the peculiar geology of northern Britain and from place names. His theory, in essence, was this: that in prehistoric times, about 4,000 to 5,000 years before Christ, northern Britain was the seat of a sophisticated and flourishing civilisation. Then, at the height of that culture a twin-headed comet appeared in the sky and, over a period of about a year, rapidly approached the earth, giving rise to rumours and terrors which persist in legend to this very day. The comet, as the wise men and priests had predicted, struck the earth in the northern hemisphere, shifting the earth's axis and destroying this northern civilisation. Certain survivors, however, had been forewarned and had fled south in front of the disaster, settling in the Mediterranean basin and giving rise to the Egyptian, Cretan and Hellenic civilisations.

'He made a fascinating comparison of place names, pointing out that names survive often long after the people who lived there have been forgotten. He compared Iona with the Ionian Sea, the Greek island of Scyros with Skye, the Hebrides with the Hesperides, the Orcades (the old name for Orkney Isles) with Arkady – and so on. But most fascinating of all was his reading of the sculptured "Pictish" stones of northern Scotland. Now these really are fascinating – and mysterious. There are hundreds of them, many in museums, many still standing in odd places throughout northern Scotland: huge, bleak monoliths which all tell the same basic tale. Most of them show at the top an inverted half-moon shape decorated with odd whorls and patterns with, underneath, twin joined orbs, sometimes called by archaeologists "the spectacles" and these are usually bisected by a zigzag, such as a child might draw to depict lightning. You'll see a number of these monoliths in any Scottish museum of note which you care to visit.

'Often, the more detailed of these stones show, beneath these symbols, what is often called a "hunting scene": carvings of men on horseback and on foot surrounded by beasts. But some of the stones show other, more enigmatic symbols, such as a ram, a serpent, a man carrying a jar, a whale and so on. Beaumont said these were Aries, Pisces, Aquarius the Water Carrier . . . and he claimed they were signs from early astrology indicating, first, the arrival in lightning and terror of the double-headed comet, the fleeing of the population from fire and flood, and the zodiacal signs giving the date of this catastrophe. He placed it some two thousand years before Christ.

'It is really a most interesting book and, in fact, though all pretend they have never heard of it, it is the seminal work in the world of arcane archaeological scholarship in which writers like Immanuel Velikovsky and Von Daniken discovered most of their original ideas – '

'Now I have heard of them,' Simon said. 'But they're just imposters, surely?'

'Of course, of course, Simon – but don't miss the point. It's not what *we* believe that matters: it's what the lunatic fringe and the romantics want to believe that counts. Von Daniken's books have sold in their millions and the only bits in them which are original are those which bear no relation to the facts.'

This was the lunatic fringe of archaeology, he explained; but it was just that gullible fringe which they needed to capture while walking the delicate balance of credibility with 'respectable' science.

The most enduring and brightest thread in the history of mankind, he said, was the desire to believe in the supernatural. Their task was to present an unorthodox, but acceptable, piece of evidence to the serious scientists and also to draw in the wider public by hinting at a larger mystery behind it. Many men, he said, before Erich Von Daniken had toyed with the idea of space-travellers visiting our earth in the past and initiating the rise of man, leaving enigmatic traces of their visit to puzzle all the succeeding generations of men. Such prophets fed on the ignorance of their listeners and on their burning need for something wonderful to transcend the mundaneness of their daily life.

'And it's not really too surprising that people should believe in Flying Saucers and Ancient Astronauts when you consider what, for the last couple of thousand years, our own Christian church would have us believe.' Who, for instance, was madder: an English lord who sat in the Second Chamber of government and who believed there was a hole in the North Pole – or was it the south one? – from which flying saucers came out to astonish mankind, or a church, endorsed by the State, which taught that two millennia ago a ghost and a woman had offspring, in or out of wedlock, in a little town in Palestine, who turned out to be the son of God? 'And that there's a god up there in the sky beyond the earth running everything from the fall of sparrows to the Red Sox versus the White Sox and that he's got a personal enemy under the earth somewhere who is frustrating his every move, called the Devil? Or that the one up there is going to give to the one down here, for his private delectation, the souls of all those who don't believe this story?

'Millions believe that, and worse, so why shouldn't they believe Mr Daniken? The odder it is, the more they're likely to believe it: whether it is the Kalahari Bushman's quaint idea that the world is run by a giant stick insect or the belief by countless thousands, now regrettably shattered, in the Loch Ness Monster.'

Simon demurred, interrupting this flow. 'But this is comic book stuff, David. What I mean – spacemen and comets and signs of the zodiac: it's all too complicated and fancy. We want something simple and effective.'

Henderson explained: he was just airing ideas. There was no question of trying to promote anything so crude as Von Daniken's absurdities. 'Nothing so idiotic as Nazca lines across the Mexican desert so the spacemen could find their way home, or Stonehenge as a sort of airport beacon. We'll just leave a faint hint of a mystery so that the nut-cases can go ride off on their hobby horses. Because there're far more of them than there are of logical men – and they're the ones who'll come to look.

'See, Simon, I believe there's a sort of gap in men's minds which used to be filled by the old mysteries and rituals of savage religion: of sacrifice and appeasement, punishment and reward.' It had turned, he said, modern half-educated men to a variety of esoteric cults and philosophies, from the Maharishis and the new Messiahs to dark old rituals of the occult and the soothsayers, while the young pranced up and down in ritualistic frenzies led by silver-suited men and girls with pouting, threatening gestures like the old African idols. 'Open the door to a belief in something strange and dark and old and beyond this earth, open it just a tiny chink and they'll burst it in and fall down and worship.'

'But surely the, er, academic archaeologists, the scientific people will just pooh-pooh all this stuff, David? They'll condemn it for the nonsense it obviously is?'

'Not so, Simon. There are a lot of odd quirks about the scientific fraternity.' It was arranged, he said, as a society within a society, in a strict and conservative hierarchy and it was fiercely and jealously competitive. A whisper of nonconformity and the pack was on to the culprit as savagely as any predator herd which senses sickness in one of its members. 'Oh, not with such blatancy, but with teeth and claws just as sharp and just as damaging. The weapons are scientific papers, lifted eyebrows, delicate corroding scorn: and chairs and grants not awarded, preferement overlooked.' So the academics dared not even refute the rubbish of the Von Danikens, the Velikovskys and the Flying Saucer time-travellers – to touch it, to deny it, is to be contaminated by it. Even to allude to it in scorn was suspect because it lent credence to the nonsense it was trying to condemn. 'It dignifies it with a denial.'

Orthodox science was, in short, terrified even to mention the esoteric offshoots of their disciplines because, having touched pitch, some of it might stick. Popularity and notoriety were nearly as dangerous as error, and popularisers of the Desmond Morris and Robert Ardrey school aroused such frenzies of jealousy within the orthodox academic milieu that they found the doors of academe slammed in their faces thereafter. 'They won't bother us at all.'

Simon shook his head and fell into a prolonged bout of ear-pulling and snuffling. 'But isn't it all a bit too . . . detailed, too sophisticated? What I mean – all this Comet Beaumont stuff, or whatever, is all rather getting away from the original concept.'

'Not really, Simon. Our original concept will stay the same and be quite simple: symbols painted on the cave walls indicating that it's the seat of some very early cult or visit, nothing more. But the *kind* of symbols we choose will allow, with a tiny bit of invisible prompting, the arcane mystery-mongers to get on with their speculations. They'll think, because they'll want to think it, that they found it all out themselves. You'll see.'

Alison, oddly enough, was more easily convinced than Simon. She had, of course, her own reasons for being involved and Henderson knew they must be pretty strong ones but he had not tried again to probe into them since the day of her arrival. He was beginning to learn what a complex self-sufficient woman this child he had once known had become. Something had happened over the years at university, at the 'digs' and field expeditions and in the back rooms of colleges and museums, which had affected her strongly and had nurtured within her an implacable desire for what looked like a revenge on the academic establishment. Had some honour been stolen from her? – it happened all too often in such circles. Had she been passed over for some preferment in some outrageously unfair way? Had her ideas been appropriated and plagiarised by some senior? He thought one of these was likely and perhaps she would tell him, perhaps she wouldn't, but he knew better than to quiz this grown-up Alison with her hard bright purposes and her outwardly cool ironic view of the world. He liked her very much and he respected what she had become. There was no doubt that she had seen through the scholarly milieu of the archaeology establishment and the hints she let fall showed that she knew its foibles and its colossal bigotries.

'You don't have to worry about getting the establishment interested,' she assured Simon, silencing his objections immediately and far more effectively than Henderson's nursings and cajolings. 'If there is some proper academically-respectable kudos to be got out of Project Cnocdruidh (as she had started calling it) then you'll have to fight them off with a sharp stick. And once they're in on it, why, Preferred End Result Syndrome will begin to operate right away. What we – most probably me – what I have to do is hint at the possibility of an important discovery to someone who's already published work on, say, pre-Pictish Scotland and the pre-eminence of early tribal nomad culture in the North in the spread of culture southwards. There's plenty of recent work on the subject and we can virtually pick and choose our stalking horse. Don't forget that the remains we're planting will test out to be very much older than anything discovered in that line so far. Oh what a flutter it's going to cause in those pompous dovecotes!' And she glanced, a co-conspirator, at David Henderson with sparkling excited eyes, giving his arm an affectionate, an intimate squeeze. She looked positively pretty at that moment.

There's something going on there, Simon thought. Ridiculous, at his age.

The next alarum was initiated by Swacky. Swacky Ross was faithful and honest. He worked occasionally for David Henderson and he liked this job, for he was a friend as well as a part-time employee: he would give him his loyalty in such measure as he deserved it and earned it. But Swacky served two masters and the other was drink. Apart from the few essentials of clothing, food and rent, he spent every other penny and most of his spare time in the pub. In this he was no different from most young men in the Highland villages who had not followed an academic or a professional career and who had not followed, either, the religion and the old-fashioned disciplines of their fathers. He put it this way: 'See, Dave, if there's nothing on the telly what's there to do at home except listen to my people going on about their aches and pains or their neighbours? In the pub there's all my friends and cronies; we swop all the news and usually the crack's good. And sometimes you meet new people.' In the big city, he implied, there were discos and cinemas, night clubs and live shows and girls: life would be very different there. In this imaginary television world there would be only excitement and glamour and problems would exist in no larger form than could be encompassed by the security of a twenty-one-inch screen. But Henderson knew that Swacky had been to the big city and after a few days of the crowds, the insecurity, the dishonesty, the violence and, above all, the anonymity, he had fled back to his quiet valley as fast as he could get there. Swacky was a man for the hills and the water, with a gill net out at midnight to reap the salmon harvest, a ferret for the rabbits and a gun for the laird's deer. There was a great deal of innocent larceny in his nature and he proved the contention that there is nothing which is half so much fun as hunting deer when the gamekeeper is hunting you.

In many ways Swacky was David Henderson's biggest asset, but he was also his biggest worry. For a start he didn't really believe in Project Cnocdruidh; he wasn't equipped by either experience or imagination to grasp entirely anything so big or, to him, abstruse. Archaeology was, to him, merely an imperfectly-understood word and that anyone could 'seed' a cave with fake archaeological remains in the way, as Henderson had tried to explain, the Klondike gold miners used to seed their useless workings with a nugget or two to raise their resale value – this was an absurd and pointless concept. He was going along with the plan because people whose learning he half-respected seemed to be serious about it and he would do his guard duty as faithfully as his character permitted, but he, who could understand very well the need for secrecy over a poaching expedition or the casting of an illegal net, could not for the life of him see the point in keeping a couple of interesting caves secret or how, by daubing the walls with drawings, you could make any money out of it. All this talk which whirled around him, about Flying Saucers, Ancient Astronauts, carbon- dating and comets, was so much moonshine. If archaeology to the Squadron Leader was as obscure as the quantum theory, to Swacky, who had never read a book in his life, it was the Wizard of Oz. And though by a great effort and in memory of the fearful oath Henderson had administered on a copy of Shakespeare's Works he could, with frequent reminders, keep quiet when he was sober, in drink the comic activities of his elders seemed merely the wanderings of men whose education had made them take leave of their senses.

And he was feeling fine, just fine. In the lounge bar of the Caledonian Hotel with lots of friends around him on a Saturday night, with six pints of Heavy and a few nips of whisky working their subtle magic around his brain — and it was his turn, it seemed to him, to entertain the company with a story. Highlanders, with the sort of delicacy unknown to their more blatant brethren further south, very rarely ask straight out for information. They merely prepare the ground for you to make your revelations by a series of hints, a concentration of interest, an oblique reference or two and a pause for you to get on with it.

Someone said: 'You're very thick these days with Briggsie and that Henderson mannie, Swack?' and shoved a whisky at him.

'Och well,' said Swacky, downing it, 'I'm helping them with a . . . a proj . . . projectile thingy, y'see an' they need my assistance.' Pride in his self-importance, hugely exaggerated by the emollient effects of the warmth and the drink, then got the better of him and he added the fatal words: 'But it's a secret, ye see, so I can't say too much about it just yet.'

Highlanders are no different from anyone else in this regard: hint that there is a breath of secrecy around and they will never rest until they have uncovered it. From then on the pressure was unremitting. There was whisky and beer, tobacco, a friendly arm over the shoulder, and a flattering sense of importance; no direct questions but nice confidence-building openers such as 'Well, Swack, if they're both paying you you must be getting rich, eh, boy?' And Swacky's increasingly fuddled replies: 'Rish, rish? No' yet, boy, but, aye, we're all going get rish at the end of it right enough.' Simon came bustling into the bar on his nightly rounds of his hotel at about this juncture and sized up the situation in a millisecond.

'Better get around here immediately,' he told Henderson on the 'phone. 'They're getting that bloody Swacky friend of yours as drunk as a skunk and he's blurting it all out.' And then he went back to fuss behind the bar in the hope that they wouldn't pump Swacky any more while he, one of the participants, was there. That would be too blatant and it was against the rules. The stratagem worked up to a point but Swacky was primed and running over; they didn't really need to pump any more, he was going to disgorge without further persuasion. He was just shouting across to Simon in a ludicrous attempt at a combined boast of his own importance and a delusion that he was being cryptic – 'Hey, Bri . . . er, Shimon, howsa PAINTING going on, eh, boy?' – as David Henderson came into the bar, ever so casually, with his blood running cold.

'Oh, hi, Simon,' he said. 'Pint of lager, if you please, and something for yourself.' And, turning around to survey the company: 'Oh, hi Geordach, Alec, Ian – hey, Swacky you bugger, you're supposed to be home with me, helping with the painting. How the hell did you manage to sneak away in here?'

Swacky sobered part way with an enormous effort which made his face bright red, the realisation of what he was doing striking him in a great wave of remorse. 'Oh, shorry, shorry, Dave,' he said, 'I shouldn't have, I shouldn' have . . . I was tellin' Geordach here about . . . about – '

'Hell, boy, it's not that secret. But you said you'd keep it quiet till it was done. Come on, I'll get you home.'

There was one last attempt by Geordach, though he knew the moment was past and yet, for all the innocence of Swacky's disclosures, he knew something was on the boil. Henderson arriving when he did and Simon hanging around the bar was too pat.

'Painting the old place, then?' he said.

Henderson grinned. 'You'll see it when it's done,' he said. 'But it would have made a nice surprise.'

And when he was gone Geordach said to the others: 'There's something. I wish I knew what. And that's the first time I've seen Davie Henderson leave his pint in the bar.'

They looked. And there it sat, bubbling gently, untouched and unpaid for, looking wrong.

CHAPTER SIX

The twin circles of the 'spectacles' with zigzag 'lightning' bisecting them – jet on a grey background – seemed to lean out of the shadows. Below them the enigmatic streamlined shape of Cetus the Whale angled upwards, a solid startling graffito against walls as old as the first crusts of earth. Off to the right, seemingly in a different and cruder style, was the towering outline of a man with wings upon his ankles and the hint of a broad brimmed hat upon his head. He was etched in an ochreous tint, deep into the granite, in profile with a great wedge of nose springing from his brow.

Alison Fraser and David Henderson sat back on their heels and surveyed the work, as fresh as the day neolithic man had daubed it on his cave wall six thousand years ago.

Henderson spoke in a sort of loud whisper, awe in his voice. 'I feel like Howard Carter,' he said, 'when he broke through the tomb of Tutankhamen and the unimaginable past rushed out and extinguished his candle. And to think that we are the first to see something much, much older: the first daubs of some hairy hunter as he crouched in terror of the night in his little sanctuary. Were there woolly mammoths outside or polar bears – or an auroch stamping on the earth with nostrils steaming –'

'Except for the small fact,' said Alison, 'that it's only six minutes old, not six millennia, and we've just done it ourselves.'

'Ah, but didn't you feel the brush taken out of your hand

at a crucial moment: something numinous and all-wise guiding us as if we were merely instruments of a Power working through us . . . ?'

Alison looked sideways at him just to make sure he was mocking. She decided he was.

'Yeah,' she said. 'The great Power of Fakery and Money. That's what I felt urging me on.'

'Me, too,' said Henderson. 'But you've got to admit it's impressive. Pity to have to spoil it.'

Because now it had to be 'aged' and abraded, scratched and sluiced with muddy water and rubbed with the deposits which they had so carefully brushed from the walls and kept in glass jars. Certain fragments of pottery and equivocally-shaped flints and other ancient detritus had to be worked into the floor to be discovered during the excavations which would follow. And then all traces of their occupancy had to be removed. 'Although,' said Alison, 'however meticulous they are – and modern archaeologists are about as careful as lab assistants working on a wonder drug – they're bound to take dust and dirt in with them when they start to dig. And they know that. If they're keen enough to make a 'find' they're prepared to ignore (even to conceal) odd bits of extraneous matter. They can always think of an explanation for something that shouldn't really be there if they want to badly enough.'

Alison, who was an impressively systematic worker, had a big chart on the wall of Henderson's study and everything to the minutest detail was noted down there in her tiny neat script, including a detailed inventory, checked at every descent and ascent, of everything they took down with them. 'I mean, they've only to find a pair of pliers, say, or a discarded ring-pull from a beer can which has rolled into a corner to realise, however much they want it to be genuine, that it hasn't come from some neolithic superstore,' she had said, sardonically. She was allowing a week for the pigments to dry, having tested them above surface on similar rock and, as carefully noted on her chart, having had her little drawings scrubbed, washed and plastered with mud to prove their survival characteristics. All was now set for the final stage of the project but time was moving on, for it was now October, and the long Highland winter was imminent, the first chilling breaths from the hills presaging snow and frost.

'Problem is,' they explained to the others at their most recent progress report, 'the longer we have to sit on it the greater is the danger of unwelcome discovery. I mean, discovery is what we want, but not by some blundering poacher like Hamish; it has to be stage-managed – and we won't be ready for that until the spring.'

There were some murmurings at this but everyone was conscious of the rigours of an East Highland winter. This was, in a typical year, signalled by the sudden breathtaking sight one morning on the surrounding hills in November of the first pure gleam of white on the high tops and a shrewd element in the wind warning of what was to come. In so ragged a terrain, with the effects of the sea and of the surrounding hills vying to create contrasting mixes of weather, there was usually no long-term pattern to the winter but from that moment when the first snow appeared on the hills it would be a broken pattern of snows and melts, frosty days of sunshine followed by cold rain, the occasional balmy day from the south-west giving way once more to increasingly severe periods of frost. It was no weather even for a hill farmer to be out if he could avoid it and a time when archaeologists would be difficult to coax from their heated studies. Nor is the British journalist a notable Spartan, prepared perhaps if it is forced upon him to make a brief foray into wellie-boot terrain but preferring to write his best fictions in a cosy room and close to a snug bar if it can possibly be arranged.

The Squadron Leader, veteran of innumerable military planning fiascos, was the least disturbed by the postponement. 'Could have told you as much,' he said. 'No plan ever worked out exactly according to timetable – you have got a timetable haven't you?' Alison assured him that they had and he nodded approvingly. 'As I'd expect from you, young lady. But security – now that's another matter. That's something we can make some hard and fast rules for and stick to them. Regular, but casual checks on the site, a total clamp-down on any loose talk, efficient routine.' And he produced in the next week an admirable little timetable of checks and times, of persons who needed to know and how much they needed to know: who should visit the site once work was complete and when those visits should occur.

The Activists, as Henderson, Alison and Simon had nominated themselves, were pleased and impressed: pleased because the Squadron Leader, while still holding himself remote from the actual physical work on the caves, had agreed to involve himself thus far and was to this extent committed, and impressed because his security system really did work and it took some of the anxiety out of the organisation.

And now the finishing stages of the cave work came to rapid completion. The nights were now longer than the days and they were able to spend many more hours in each twenty-four at the site, all in conformity with the Squadron Leader's carefully worked-out plans. The 'ageing' and partial concealment of the rock wall painting was done in a week, and in less than a week of nights after that, Alison, with minimal help from David Henderson, had buried her other treasures. There came a night when, with Swacky's help, they rolled a big rock over the entrance heavy enough so no one man could remove it and, amid intermittent sleet showers and glimpses of a thin moon, they left the hill for the last time until the spring. And when Swacky had gone off down the road home, Alison and Henderson sat up very late before a big log fire, not saying much to each other but with gloom and a kind of hopelessness which seemed in harmony with the dying year settling on them. Eventually he said: 'The swallows have all gone south, Ally and the snow's coming. You're pluming for flight too, I guess?'

She came and sat close by his side. 'How did you know, Davie?'

'I've known for a week. More than a week. Really, I suppose, since that night when we finished the painting.'

She said: 'How could you have known? I didn't. But, yes, you are right, I do have to go. There was once or twice when I almost . . . I nearly . . . Oh hell – I just have to go. D'you want to know why?'

'I don't want you to tell me,' he said, 'in case I don't like the answer. Just so long as you come back in the spring.'

'Oh yes,' she said, and kissed him very affectionately. 'Before the swallows – about the same time as the cuckoo.'

And as the days shortened and the winter's grip tightened daily, David Henderson might well have slipped into a sort of numbed hibernation had it not been, some few weeks later, for the violent eruption on to the scene of a new and disturbing element. It came without any warning whatever in the form of a voice on the telephone which said in the unmistakable tones of the American mid-West: 'David Henderson? Well, Hi. I'm Caleb Jefferson. I'm told you're the man to see about that hill of yours – *Karnak* is it?'

'Cnocdruidh,' Henderson said, 'and it's — '

'Yeah, *Karnak*, that's it. I'm interested in buying a piece of it and building on it and someone said I ought to speak to you before getting in touch with Dickinson, the owner. Is it OK for me to call round and visit with you?'

Henderson told him to come around right away and sat there holding the telephone after Jefferson had broken the connection, feeling, as he told Simon later, as if he had trodden in the dark on a stair that wasn't there. There was the same feeling of a sudden loss of confidence and the certain knowledge that something painful was to follow. He had heard of Caleb Jefferson, had even seen him at a distance, but had not met him. He was one of that small but growing band of successful middle-aged American businessmen with roots some generations back in the Highlands who sought to enrich their lives by re-staking a small claim for part of every year in the land which had thrown out their great grandparents to starve or survive in Canada, the United States, Africa, Australia and other places which they had duly colonised with their sweat and ingenuity and an imperfectly-recalled tradition. Caleb Jefferson, he had heard, though, was not one of those who was content to spend his vacationing weeks walking the hills, fishing the rivers and buying up Victorian 'antiques' – Jefferson was a doer, a disrupter, a bulldozer and a builder, a dynamo of a man, big and boisterous and brimful of energy. In his mind's eye, Henderson could see the surveyors with their little barbers' poles and theodolites swarming over Cnocdruidh planting their little markers, and the throb of the earth-movers as they gathered their energies to bring a terrible order to wild disorder and to make the rough places plain.

Jefferson arrived thirty minutes later in a battered Land Rover, sprayed gravel over Henderson's front windows, and bustled out, hand-outstretched, dressed in a sort of Alaskan parka and a fur hat, looking as huge and disruptive as a grizzly bear. He had a big grin, with a lot of very white teeth, and a loud cheerful voice. He made Henderson's sitting room look small and he opened negotiations by pulling a bottle of rare old malt whisky from one of the many pockets of his parka.

'A dram first, talk later,' he said and poured two huge measures into the tubby glasses Henderson set out on the table. He took a big gulp, said in a passable accent, 'Here's tae us,' set the glass down and turned and stared through the big picture window at the looming mass of Cnocdruidh over which the winter darkness was rapidly gathering.

'Yep,' he said. 'Yep. One hell of a fine site for a restaurant and bar, with chalets, maybe, placed here and there among those patches of birch. Won't need to tear the place up too much, I guess: just a bit of landscaping and an access road. Maybe a "hide" halfway up for bird and deer watching. Perhaps one of those artificial ski-slopes to keep the youngsters happy. I hear there's a cave there, too. Maybe we could make a feature of that.'

And then, as Henderson stared at that broad plaid-clad back in utter despair, he saw the big shoulders start to shake and when Caleb Jefferson turned around again to face him he saw that he was shaking with silent laughter which burst out in a roar as he saw the despair on his face. A hand came out and clapped him on the shoulder. 'Christ,' Caleb said, 'your face, man. Aw Gee, I'm sorry, but I couldn't resist it.' He held out the big hand again and said: 'Look, call me Cal – what sort of a name is Caleb, anyway? – and count me in. I want to join your little group. Your secret's safe with me.'

'What secret? What group? Who – who've you been talking to?'

Henderson didn't really know what he was saying; he needed time to think and plan. This bluff frontal approach was something he had not envisaged.

Cal said: 'I know it was a lousy trick to wind you up like that, Dave, but it seemed a good idea at the time. Truth is: I keep my ear pretty well pressed to the railroad track and I heard rumblings, oh, a month ago that something was going on up this here hill. Now I'm looking for some little business to get involved in while I'm here, you see, to keep me busy and it's my habit to check the ground very carefully before I go in for something. Not literally,' he added, hastily, when he caught the expression on Henderson's face. 'But it's quite simple, really. Hamish Matheson is cutting wood and odd-jobbing around my place and when he failed to turn up one day I asked him why, and he told me about his terrible experience on the hill. Now I don't believe in ghosties and devils even if Hamish does and the whole thing reminded me about something I once read about the Klondikers – about seeding useless mines with nuggets to trick some dude into buying them. Well, it was obvious to me you'd found something and equally obvious you weren't about to come and tell me about it – so here I am. So what have you found there, huh? It ain't gold, and it ain't diamonds and it sure as hell ain't oil and it's been driving me crazy trying to work out what it is.' He drained his whisky – it didn't seem to have any effect on him, although Henderson was already feeling a bit light-headed – and poured them both another. And then he sat, quite quiet, and waited. There is a terrible power in silence, something about it which makes even the strongest-minded want to fill it, to bridge it, with talk, or action, or noise of any kind. Cal knew this power and sat and let it work for him.

David Henderson took a good long speculative look at this large and boisterous American. He was such an archetype of the brash Yank of fiction and popular journalism that it was hard to see through the facade to the real person, the mind was so confused by cliché and by legend. What made an assessment more difficult was that so many products, like Cal, of that vast and romantic culture followed the cliché and acted out the part they had invented for themselves. Henderson believed he could see, however, beneath this carapace a man more familiar to European eyes: a clever and highly intelligent man who confronted the world head-on and with a certain boyish enthusiasm which, nonetheless, did not betoken childishness or immaturity – this show was, so to speak, only the bow-wave pushed out in front of a powerful personality. He weighed him as best he could and judged him discreet and so he told him. He told him of the economic plight of the area – which Cal knew about – and of their luck in finding the Caves – which he did not know about – and the use to which they had put them and what they hoped the result would be. He told him everything and a couple of times during the telling Cal slapped his knee and burst out with various objurgations of 'Wheeow!' and the more conventional 'Gee!' and finally 'Keerist!' His face was flushed and excited when Henderson finished and his bright blue eyes were sparkling with glee, and he poured out another two hefty shots of the malt whisky, raised his glass to Henderson in salute and before drinking said: 'That's about the neatest bit of fraud I've ever heard of – and I don't even think they could get you for it if they found out. What laws does it break after all – the advertising code, the Sale of Goods Act? – and I congratulate you most sincerely. How the hell did you get the Squadron Leader to go along with you? And the hotelier? And Dickinson? He sounds like a stuffed shirt to me.'

Well, the Squadron Leader wasn't too sure, still wasn't too sure, but the public utilities and the elected and non-elected officials had made him so angry by their deceits and prevarications that he had begun to question the bases of the world by which he had, until now, lived and given him a sort of manumission – to challenge the foundations of that world and, if he could not make them conform to reason, to attack them. It was the very stuff of revolution, and, like all the successful revolutions in history, it had its birth in the educated middle-class. Simon Briggs was a much simpler creature. He was obsessed with money. And Monty Dickinson was, indeed, a stuffed shirt who didn't really have the brains to understand what was going on. Fortunately he was a man whose actions were fairly easy to predict, for he was powerfully motivated by a single overwhelming desire: to become what he imagined was an English gentleman. Provided the enterprise could be fitted into that picture he had of himself he would cooperate to the limit of his abilities.

Cal nodded his head at all this. 'We have exactly the same types back home. They're just called by different names.' And then he confessed that his approach to Henderson was not entirely a fiction. 'I've got an option on those old farm buildings down the road,' he said, 'and I've been turning over in my mind what to do with them. I had thought of a horseback riding centre or an adventure centre but now I think, with your Caves potential, I'll turn it into a restaurant, hotel and bar. Think I'll get any grief from the county government?'

Henderson told him he'd have to fight every inch of the way. It was a conundrum he'd never been able to solve: the public pronouncements of local politicians who called for development and employment and the series of hurdles and traps which they then placed in the way of anyone who took them up on it.

'Same again in my country,' said Cal. 'But I guess they don't get away with it back home quite so easy. Still, there are plenty ways of shifting these assholes if you know how.' (Then and for the rest of their acquaintance Henderson was amazed by the number of different permutations Cal could ring with the word 'ass', adapting it for a bewildering variety of occasions and descriptions which argued for a certain national cultural obsession with the anal sphincter which might well provide a fruitful field of study for some American Ph D student of psychology.) He had nothing but enthusiasm, however, for Cal's enterprise and wished him well in his inevitable fight with planning and licensing authorities. The ensuing discussions became progressively more dispersed as the level in the whisky bottle sank for it was not until it was entirely finished that Cal took his leave, seemingly quite unaffected by half a bottle of extra strong spirits as Henderson, under a cold clear sky which wheeled and span with frosty stars, waved him away from his door.

Over the next week Henderson saw a lot of Cal and grew to like and respect the big boisterous American. And there was one more unscheduled night-time visit to the Cnocdruidh Caves, for Cal was undisguisedly frantic to see them and to place another artifact beneath the floor which he and Henderson had prepared, after getting Alison's approval. The impression of awe which the Caves had on Cal, even though he knew the paintings were fakes and even though he was prepared for what he saw, had a quieting effect on the extroverted American which was more deeply impressive than all his enthusiastic outpourings and which gave Henderson huge encouragement that there would be a similar reception when they were opened, finally, to the world. Cal went absolutely quiet for several minutes, examining the graffiti in great close-up detail and said, finally, in a hushed voice: 'This, man, is really something. You and that girlfriend of yours, Davie, are geniuses, geniuses. It's better, even, than I imagined.'

But, Henderson wanted to know, would it bring the public in?

'You can bet your sweet ass it will,' Cal said.

Once during that long winter, the longest he could remember, when everything outside was so deep in snow-wrapped silence that the house might have been covered to the very roof in a drift of snow, Henderson thought: we've planted the seeds and planted them deep. Now it must lie dormant like everything else in this winter land until the frosts are past and the new germination begins. And I wonder, how I wonder, what that springing will be like. Am I wrong? Is Cal wrong? Will no-one pay the least attention to our mystery? For all our planning and care will some expert just take a quick look at it and burst out laughing at the joke? Can we really expect to fool the experts and, even if we do, will the people come to see?

Similar thoughts seemed to be afflicting his landlord. Monty Dickinson, while playing virtually no part in the whole enterprise, nevertheless felt himself to have some responsibility for it. The others had only brought him in because, apart from being a big man in the district, the Caves were on his land. As Henderson explained to him: 'If we could have found them anywhere else, Monty, we would have done but we didn't have any choice. They're there, that's all. You shouldn't own so bloody much of the countryside. But what's that land worth – an acre or two of peat, heather and rock? Five hundred pounds? A thousand, if you're lucky. You'll be able to sell it to the Society for the Preservation of Ancient Monuments, or some such, for twenty thousand. Or put a car park on it, or a restaurant. Go into business like us other peasants and sell tickets and teas and videos. Time you did something for a living instead of just pulling in rent money for crumbling old houses.' (This was a sore point, for Henderson's house needed paint, it needed slates, it needed renovation and he believed it was the landlord's duty to see to these things in return for his rent.) But Monty Dickinson, despite his ownership of several thousand acres of hill and grazing and deer forest, was as short of money as the rest of them and mortgaged, bound, promised and borrowed up to the limits the usurers would allow. Characteristically, though, what worried him more than money were the ethics of the project. 'Dammit, I was a public school boy,' he protested idiotically, 'and a captain in the Army. I can't make money out of a fraud.' Only just able to suppress his laughter Henderson tried to explain as well as he could that Monty need make no claims at all for the authenticity of the Caves. He could, if this would mollify his public school conscience, even express doubts about the authenticity of the paintings, within reason; and then he could with a clear mind take the money from the Ancient Monuments Trust, or whatever, if they wanted to give him a thousand times what he had paid for his miserable field. 'And you do need the money, Monty, to fix up the houses of your tenants, some of whom are collecting the drips from the roofs in buckets.'

Monty was not so easily fobbed off, however. A man with very few ideas, when he had one he tended to stick to it. He nagged and picked and worried at the subject, perhaps enjoying the sense of importance it gave him and the chance of associating with cleverer people; and he certainly enjoyed the luxury of agonising over the morals of making a huge profit for nothing. He was a man of unpredictable moods, though, and was giving

David Henderson a great deal of unnecessary worry because he was quite capable, if attacked by a sudden access of puritanism, of sabotaging the entire ploy. But one night, not long after Alison had gone, he turned up at Henderson's home looking a lot happier. 'I was talking to Hugh – Hugh Ross – about it all,' he said, 'and he's given me some sound advice. He said the best thing I could do is make sure I'm not seen to be associated with the thing at all and not to be here when it all happens. And so it happens that an old uncle of mine has died out East and left a bit of property in Ceylon. So I've decided to go out there and attend to the details – stay on a while during the winter here.' And he was, indeed, off on the first plane available.

Another one gone South for the winter, Henderson thought. But this one did not leave a void behind him. He really hardly noticed he had gone.

THE SPRING

CHAPTER SEVEN

His pinkly-bald head looking strangely vulnerable with its baby fuzz of hair above the ears, Dr Nathaniel Mould descended the ladder into the side of Cnocdruidh Hill. Once below he called for more light and a camping gas lamp was sent down to him on a cord. A further pause and his voice came up, echoey and sepulchral, complaining that he had turned the thing on and that it was making a hissing noise but no light was coming out. 'Christ,' said his assistant, 'he'll blow himself up,' and he hollered down the hole for his chief to turn it off again at once.

Swacky said to David Henderson: 'I think he's no' too bright, himself. Are you certainsure they've got the right man?'

Swacky's doubts about Dr Mould's intelligence were understandable. Even among his colleagues Mould was something of an enigma and, like some other brilliant individuals, an odd bundle of contradictions. The very concentration of mind which had made him into such a fine scholar, a faculty of seeing his object of study in close magnification, excluding all distractions, had the side-effect of making him dottily unaware of everything else that was going on around him. And while he could be childishly humble before a plumber working what was, to him, magic over something so simple as a ball-cock valve, on his own subject and among his colleagues and students his arrogance knew no bounds. And like many another academic, while he was honest to a fault about money and taxes and truth-telling, when it came to the advancement of his scholarly career he had the morals of a guttersnipe and the proclivities of a whore. No-one else's work was sacrosanct and his effrontery in appropriating others' ideas and research was breathtaking. He was, in short, an academic psychopath. There were those who maintained that the main corpus of his work on the rise and spread of neolithic communities in Britain was a brilliant mix appropriated from the work of others, with a series of unwarranted assumptions based on facts which were by no means proven. None said it to his face, however, and none said it quite so baldly. He was surrounded by half-hints and scholarly head-shakings – although this, in what is a necessarily speculative discipline, is by no means unusual.

Alison Fraser in several letters to Henderson during the winter had described how she had got the great man interested in the Cnocdruidh site. As a postgraduate student of his she had approached him about a study she was making of sculptured standing stones in the Scottish Highlands and the difficulty she was experiencing in dating these which had been overlaid during the early Christian era by the Celtic cross. In many cases the missionary monks had obliterated all but a tiny portion of the original pictograms, in others they had merely superimposed the Cross and yet others, of which the Golspie Stone was a supreme example, had been left untouched. This deliberate overlaying of the original symbols by missionary monks was the clearest indication, she argued, that these monoliths were important objects of worship by the native population of that time – for it was the custom of the missionaries everywhere to replace pagan creeds both physically and spiritually by their own – and logic would dictate that these were, therefore, potent symbols of great meaning. Had they been put there by the population which worshipped them or, as would seem more likely, had they been left by an even earlier culture and thus stood as objects of legend and veneration even then? She was interested and puzzled by the recurrent symbolism of the 'spectacles' and lightning, the inverted moon, the fish and other figures and shapes which were displayed in one way or another not merely by a dozen or a score but on literally hundreds of these huge stones. If, as current interpretation would have it, they were merely hunting scenes or scenes of battle, why did they portray the same scene every time – and why, in that case, were they worshipped? And, when she had his interest, she let it slip that, while she was on holiday in the far north during the past summer, she had heard rumours of a cave, certainly not recorded in any study, in which these same symbols were said to have been seen. She had even been shown the spot where it was thought to be but had been unable to investigate owing to the lateness of the year and the uncertainty of the whole thing.

'He's hooked,' she wrote to Henderson. 'In the most casual way possible the devious old swine has got the name of the village and even a more-or-less accurate address of your place, out of me. He says, in a sort of weary off-hand way that perhaps, next summer, he and I might make a trip that way and perhaps, if there's time, take a look at my rumoured place. At any rate I'm to remind him of it sometime nearer the next summer vacation, in case he forgets all about it. But the greedy old sod will be up there as soon as the snow melts, you can bet your old wellie boots: and he'll just somehow forget to mention it to me. Oh, how I'm enjoying this!'

Dr Mould had planned his arrival rather cleverly, but it is hard for those whose natural milieu is the big city to comprehend just how closely-knit the Highland communities are: rather like a huge extended family. Thus, when he booked rooms in a hotel which he judged to be near enough to Cnocdruidh and yet not so near as to excite curiosity, and when he sent his young assistant out to poke around the area and casually to engage David Henderson in conversation on his doorstep, how could he have known that his host, Simon Briggs, was Henderson's friend and co-conspirator or that Alison Fraser had told her old teacher the day and hour he was coming? Or that the arrival of Swacky Ross while Henderson and the assistant were talking was carefully contrived and not the lucky chance that it seemed? So when Henderson asked Swacky to show the young man up the hill to see the hole in the ground where he had lost his ferret, it seemed merely the friendly act of a stranger and the most natural thing in the world.

'Skinny little fellow, thon,' Swacky reported later when the assistant, who was trying to look calm and unimpressed by what he had seen, and not making a convincing job of it, had departed to liaison with his master. 'There's more meat on a bicycle frame than on him. I got him to help me push the stone away from the hole and for all the help he was, it might have been a midgie pushing at it. We got it moved right enough though and down he goes on his hands and knees in the glaur and shines his torch in. And then he goes dead still for a minute, like a whippet that's seen a rabbit. I could hear him muttering to himself real excited-like. And then he comes backing out all in a dither. "Have you been down there?" he asks in that funny accent of his. I tells him No, like you told me to, but I tells him I shined a torch in it just like him, last year, when I lost the ferret. "Did you see anything?" he asks. I mean, what sort of a fool question is that? So I says Yes. He says "What?" and I says stones and earth and rock but no sign of a damned ferret. "And that's all?" he says. Well, there was a lot of rabbit shit and roots and some marks on the walls, I says, as near as I could make out – but nothing worth going down there for. "What sort of marks?" Well, you know, marks. Like someone gouged a circle out, or part of a circle – but you often see that marks on stones hereabouts and maybe no-one made them and they just got there natural. "D'you tell anyone else about it?" he says, sort of nervous-like. And I says I sort of mentioned it to you and you said we must have a look at it some day – but we never did. And then he says "Right, Mr Ross, now can I rely on you not to bring anyone else here till I've brought a friend of mine to have a look?" And I says, Well, if someone, say a friend, like, asks how can I refuse? And he gives me this.' 'This' was a £5 note. 'I reckon there's more where that came from.'

Henderson assured him that there was. And so it turned out.

And now here they were on the following day with the little assistant whom Swacky insisted on calling 'Midgie' from then on, but who in reality was named Ryle, once more in a panic as he disappeared down the ladder after his master, urgently willing him not to strike a light. 'Christ,' he was saying as he slithered down, 'Christ all-bloody-mighty, don't let him have any matches.' And it was ten minutes before he judged the place to be gas-free and permitted the lamp to be lit – ten minutes in which the two men explored by torchlight. The brilliant flare of the camping light when it was eventually lit was followed by another long pause below. When Dr Mould came puffing up to the surface about an hour after they had gone down they were in a curious mixture of solemnity and suppressed excitement. They were trying very hard to preserve an outward show of calmness, much like a bidder at an auction who has set his heart on an object which he earnestly desires but is putting on an air of sangfroid for his competitors. It had the curious effect that they would start to say something quite ordinary and then tail off into silence as the wonderment of what they had seen would snatch their thoughts away. All Dr Mould would say about what they had seen, though, was: 'There's something down there, don't know what yet, but it merits investigation. First thing we have to do . . . ' and his mind and his eye wandered off to some remote place for about ten seconds and then his eye focused again and he gave a little start like a man who has been awoken from sleep. 'Er,' he said, 'er – '

'You were saying that the first thing you had to do was something or other,' Henderson prompted.

'Ah, yes. First thing we have to do is secure the site. That means getting in touch with the landowner – know who he is?' He took out a notebook and started to write down Monty Dickinson's name and address and stopped again, in mid-dictation, pencil stilled, still staring at the page but not seeing it. Henderson gently took the book out of his hand and wrote it down for him while he pulled himself back again from wherever he had gone.

'Er, thanks,' he said. 'Oh yes . . . And this is absolutely vital: we must ensure that no-one goes down there without authorisation. Now I wonder,' he looked at Henderson, then Swacky, made his choice, 'if we can make a temporary arrangement with, say, Mr Ross here to stand unofficial guard over the place in case others have noticed us here. Until we can fix up proper arrangements. Prevent anyone with hare-brained ideas about treasure-hunting and so on despoiling the place? It has happened. Terrible, irretrievable damage has been done in the past. Thing is to make clear that whatever's down there . . . ' He stopped again for a few seconds. 'Excuse me – what was I saying?'

'Whatever's down there.'

'Yes, whatever's down there. Yes, er – whatever it is – and we haven't really got much of a clue yet – it's not worth anything, except to an archaeologist. Can we rely on you, Mr Ross – for a small retainer of course?' And when Henderson had explained what a retainer was, Swacky was all for it. A few minutes later they stood together watching Dr Mould and Ryle making their way back down the hill to the road again. They stopped many times and there was a lot of gesturing and nodding, but they finally reached the road and their car without mishap. Swacky was staring at them in astonishment.

'What the hell's the matter with them?' he said. 'D'you think they've been supping on a gillock flask down there, or something?'

No, Henderson explained, as far as he knew they didn't have a flask of anything down there: it was excitement at what they saw.

'What? That pictures you and Ally did? Man, they must be gey easily excited.' And when Henderson tried to explain he listened but clearly didn't believe.

'Oh, I'll take your word for it,' Swacky said. And then, thinking of his retainer: 'I told you there was money in it,' as if Henderson had ever denied it.

Negotiations with Dickinson, or his agents, must have gone smoothly for within twenty-four hours a substantial fence was being erected around the site with a gate to which Dr Mould and Swacky had the keys. And for the next week the doctor and his assistant spent at least twelve hours a day underground and information about their progress, being reported on and interpreted by Swacky, was necessarily rather limited.

'They was awful excited this morning,' he reported to

Henderson on the third or fourth day. 'I stuck my head down the hole but all I could hear was something about a shirt, at least it sounded like a shirt but with they English accents it's hard to tell what they're saying. Would someone have left a shirt down there?'

Henderson explained about sherds, potsherds, bits of broken pottery from long ago.

'Aye. Well. That's what they were on about. Fair excited, too. The astrologist mannie, he said he thought it was from early pally-or-something times and it was earlier – does that make sense? – than any other shirts he'd found up here. Then there was a lot of stuff about the drawing on the wall which I couldn't rightly follow and the young lad, Midgie – Ryle you call him – he reckoned it was real old – a couple of thousand years maybe, but not as old as the shirt – but the old bodach, he didn't think it was as old as that. I wish I could have set them straight and told them how you and Alison only made it last year – '

'Don't you even contemplate it, Swacky – '

'Oh, I'm no' daft, man. But it's great seein' two such solemn buggers arguin' and fighting with each other and all the time you and Ally have got them fooled good and proper.'

'I hope so, Swacky, I hope so. But there's a long way to go yet. Fingers crossed and mouths shut, eh?'

The frustrating thing about Swacky as a source of information was a combination of his total ignorance of the subject and his desire to please. When he didn't hear clearly some snippet of information which he judged to be of importance he was very liable to substitute some inspired guesswork for the lacuna. Thus he had Henderson in a state of total alarm when he reported one day that Dr Mould had told Ryle that he had discovered that the cave's contents were 'artificial'. And it was only after much careful examination and cross-examination that the word Swacky had overheard turned out to be 'artefact'. 'Oh, dammit, I was only one wee bitty out,' he grumbled when Henderson got impatient with him.

Tension, though, was building up and Henderson had to admit to himself that anxiety was making him short-tempered and over-imaginative. When the archaeologists were quiet, was it because they had discovered the fraud? When they were noisy, had Swacky reported them correctly? And why had they shown no excitement about the inner cave where they had drawn their winged and hatted figure? Had he and Alison covered their work too carefully? He telephoned her after several days of this, unable to bear the strain by himself any longer. She listened, hardly saying a word, until he ran down. There was a longish silence. She said: 'I should be there with you. It's not fair on you, and I know it. But we know why I can't be there: they're bound to wonder if I had anything to do with it. But, David, believe me, you really don't have to worry. They will, literally, go over every square millimetre and they're bound to find our figure. I mean, it's nearly nine feet high. They'd find a match-head if we'd left one down there. But they're very systematic, working their way in slowly, slowly, noting down every inch they progress. Don't worry. It's just a question of time. They'll probably find it tomorrow.'

And it was on the next day, just as if Alison had known, that the breakthrough came and the reaction of Dr Mould and Ryle was absolutely unmistakable. Swacky's erratic reporting was not required; he and Henderson knew by their solemnised and silent demeanour when they came out of their hole into the daylight an hour earlier than usual that the archaeologists had made a discovery of outstanding importance. They were pale, uncertain in their movements, a little awed by what they had been looking at for the last hour and very, very quiet. All Dr Mould would say as they tidied up for the day was: 'We have made a discovery which may shed new light on the interpretation of palaeolithic man and his migrations. There is something down there so valuable that we must make immediate arrangements to safeguard it and then get a preliminary report out . . . ' He seemed a bit dazed, disorientated, and not fully aware to whom he was talking; he was really talking to himself while his imagination was leaping ahead to the lectures he would be delivering and the papers he would write – perhaps the important posts he would be asked to fill and how best it should be presented in the definitive account which he would be asked to publish. How best to make the public announcement? Should he confine himself to one of the more serious Sunday newspapers? He would have to clear all this with museum and university authorities and superiors . . . that man Henderson was saying something.

'Sorry, what?'

Henderson said again: 'You'll need a special guard on it then? In case word gets around, I mean, the way it has a habit of doing in a place like this – and in case you get sightseers trying to go down there.'

That idea pulled Dr Mould back with a sudden and unpleasant immediacy into the jejune world of petty annoyances, of ignorant amateurs seeking treasure, of the world of dim and impeding officialdom. He was afflicted by an ambivalence which had dogged him for many a year: the need for public and academic recognition and the necessity of keeping new discoveries secret for as long as it took to analyse them and accumulate data. It was an agonising dilemma, for the more popular recognition he won the more scorn would be heaped upon him from the jealous academic hierarchy of his science. Paradoxically, that hierarchy which held the keys of the doors marked Preferment and Appointment, Nathaniel Mould yearned for and to which he had directed all his energies since he first planned out his career – that hierarchy, while affecting to despise popular appeal in archaeology was, in reality, deeply influenced by it. For in the end it is politicians who decide which grants and how much universities and other institutions receive and politicians are deeply and irrevocably committed to popularity. So Mould had to conceal his find and extol it, keep it under wraps and bruit it to the world, be discreet and brash all at the same time if he wished to extract the maximum benefit and recognition from it. He knew, therefore, that there was endless trouble a-brewing as there always was when some important discovery was made, but the first thing he had to be sure of was the security of the Cnocdruidh Caves. He was grateful that Henderson had jogged him into action. There was a routine to follow in these cases but there were no hard and fast sets of rules; it was based, like the common law, on goodwill, general acceptance, good sense and precedent: one of those British compromises in which the cooperation of the local authorities and the police was essential. First he placed Swacky on his official imprest account of payments. Then he asked David Henderson, as the nearest resident to the Caves, to keep a supervisory eye on the whole thing for the next few weeks and to let him know immediately if there was any breach of what he called 'the integrity' of the site. (Henderson noted with wry amusement the class-distinction inherent in this arrangement which ruled that whereas Swacky was to be paid a respectable retainer, his responsibility for overseeing the site was to be left to the promptings of his own conscience as an educated and socially-responsible citizen.) Dr Mould explained: 'I have to report back to the faculty, the museum and our trustees on the preliminary examination I've made so that I can get a provisional funding for security and expenses for the first exploration. It's the most dangerous time in any archaeological discovery when there's not enough evidence to plead for a big outlay and yet a site of inestimable value can be destroyed by sensation-seekers or even' — and he looked quite murderous for so scholarly a man — 'treasure hunters. The trouble is that television and some sorts of journalism have made archaeology, or the fringe aspects of it, too damned popular altogether.'

Henderson said he would do his best to ensure there was no vandalism of that kind at the Caves, but he advised Dr Mould that he would be wise to consult the local police.

'Of course, of course,' the doctor said impatiently, 'but even that carries its dangers, you know. Archaeology to the average policeman carries the stamp of a Slightly Dotty but Harmless Hobby. It is therefore treated with tolerant amusement but not taken very seriously. It would be different if I could tell them there was a chest full of doubloons or silver objects down there. After all, if there's no ancient treasure down there it can't be worth much, can it? If it's not worth putting in a bank or taking away to be sold, the constabulary finds it almost impossible to believe it's worth protecting. And of course since it goes down on the police day-by-day report it's the sort of thing they pass on to the local newspaper – and after that, who knows?' He waved his little pink hands in the air as if he were shooing away something indescribably unpleasant. 'What exaggerations! What fancies, what wild speculations, misquotations, misreportings! I have known of careers, promising careers, permanently damaged by one injudicious word to an ignorant reporter.'

He went fussing off to issue Swacky with his last instructions and Henderson and the assistant were left standing together in silence. Henderson decided to take a leaf out of Caleb's book and, although he was as susceptible as anyone to a prolonged awkward silence he forced himself to stand perfectly still and watch Ryle, unspeaking. The young man fidgeted, shifted his feet about, said, finally: 'He gets a bit worked up when he comes across something as important as this. He worries about damage being done and premature stories getting out.'

'Is it that important?' Henderson said.

'If it's as good as it looks at first glance you're going to find yourself right next door to one of the major finds of this century, Mr Henderson. I can't say any more than that – it's too early. But. You know.'

There was another longish silence while Henderson, enjoying himself, stood as still as he could, saying absolutely nothing. After considerable displacement activity (scratching the tip of one ear, pulling his nose, looking up at the sky, prodding the earth with the toe of his Wellington boot) Ryle said: 'You see, we found something pretty remarkable in the inner cave. We've – or, rather, Dr Mould – never seen anything quite like it before in Britain. The central figure is quite amazing and is bound to attract a lot of speculation.'

Henderson judged it safe to speak. 'How do you present your evidence? Do you have photographs, for instance?'

'Um. And sketches. And some material for carbon-dating. All this will take months of work, which is why the old man is beginning to get anxious about the site. The public must be kept out of it at all costs . . . '

CHAPTER EIGHT

Don Eglinton was the Inverness 'stringer' for a famous Sunday newspaper. A 'stringer' is a professional reporter, usually employed on the staff of a provincial weekly or daily newspaper, who is entrusted to keep the 'national' for which he holds the string in touch with such news as occurs in his area which is sensational enough or important enough to demand a larger audience than his own parish. If he is a particularly valuable source he is put on a retainer, which is a monthly sum of sufficient size to keep him faithful to one 'national' and only one and persuade him not to try to play one off against another. His value increases in proportion to his treachery to the local newspaper which employs him full-time, for he must withhold from it whatever he sends to the big newspaper he strings for. If he is very well thought of he is often allowed to investigate and write unimportant stories himself for the big national newspaper. These, however, hardly ever appear in the patron newspaper in anything like the shape they receive them in; they are cooked, seasoned, spiced and squeezed into unrecognisable shapes before appearing for the public to read. But more often the stringer is a mere tip-off man who alerts the London journal he has sold his allegiance to, and which then sends one of its own staff to write up the yarn.

Eglinton, though, had been given his head on this one and, rightly, he saw in this commission his chance to leave the increasingly dull world of the provinces and win his place in that Hollywood of all British journalists, London. To achieve that aim he was prepared to bend every last effort towards writing a story with impact and drama. When he pulled the old-fashioned brass bell cord on David Henderson's front door and heard the bell ring within, he did not have to send to know for whom it tolled: it was tolling for him. He would have been a great deal less worried, though, had he known that he was part of a benign conspiracy and that his success was virtually guaranteed, for he had been set up, primed and pointed in the right direction by Henderson himself. He had telephoned Eglinton's office secretary himself with news of the Cnocdruidh Caves' discovery. Using a trick he had learned long ago at the receiving end of public relations experts' wiles, he had implied that the discovery at Cnocdruidh was a secret which its nearest neighbour was most anxious to keep concealed. He knew that there is no surer way to achieve publicity than to pretend that publicity is the last thing you're looking for. Government and big business have long used the same psychological trick by leaking the very information which they are anxious to see exposed, in the pretence that it has been handed to one small privileged group of reporters by a defector who is breaching a top secret. Henderson had never known the device to fail and here was Eglinton ringing his doorbell, proving its efficacy once again.

If the law which states that, other things being equal, a man will succeed in a competitive world in direct ratio to his physical defects and deformities has even a germ of truth in it, Henderson thought, Don Eglinton was destined to reach the top of his profession. He was as short as Napoleon, as ugly as Cromwell and as preposterous as Mussolini. There was more than a passing resemblance to the first Lord Beaverbrook. What he may have lacked in intellect he more than made up for in energy. He was constantly in motion and even when he sat in repose was a drummer of fingers, a tapper of feet and a scratcher of nose and scalp. His opening gambit, while still standing on Henderson's doorstep, was: 'Mr Henderson? Mr Henderson, what's all this about hiding a treasure-trove in your back garden?'

David Henderson gave a delighted chuckle and took Eglinton's arm and drew him into the house, put him into a comfortable chair and fetched him a glass of beer. 'Very nicely done, my boy,' he said. 'If I hadn't used that approach myself a few times you would have had me twitching and stammering on my own doorstep. You see, I used to be in your line of business myself a long time ago. Just tell me how I can help you and what you want to know.'

Eglinton was not one for subtleties and ornamentation: he went for his subject with the sort of heroic insensitivity which Henderson had met with more commonly in door-to-door salesmen and canvassing politicians. And he seemed to be ideal for Henderson's purposes, for he seemed to know absolutely nothing about archaeology, almost nothing of early history and on subjects such as simple chemistry and physics and carbon-dating he was as ignorant as a Kalahari bushman. On this tabula rasa one could write whatever one chose, provided you made Eglinton think he had divined it himself by his own wits and energies.

The simplest procedure was to hand Eglinton over to Swacky Ross, after carefully briefing them both. 'Don't try to tell him anything,' he told Swacky, 'just let him bribe you into letting him inside the fence and down into the Caves. And don't worry about asking him for too much; it's not him that'll be paying but the publishers of the wretched comic he's working for. And I hear they're not short of a penny or two. Just tell him you'll probably lose the first job you've ever had and ask him for the equivalent of a month's wages. He'll probably offer you half, but he'll be glad to give you the other half when he sees what's down there and gets his pictures of it.' All this sounded pretty good to Swacky who had never thought more than a month ahead in his whole life.

Preparing Eglinton was a little more difficult. He had to believe that his invasion of the caves was a brilliant *coup* and not something which Henderson devoutly wished for and had manipulated him into. He told the reporter before handing him over to Swacky: 'I'm only helping you because you seem to know about this already from some source or another and because all this secrecy goes against the grain with me. I suppose it's something to do with the years I, myself, spent as a journalist. I mean, the authorities are so habituated to denying things and concealing things that half the time they're hiding things that would actually be to their credit, don't you think? Just you make your arrangements with young Swacky, er, Alec Ross. I'm sure if you offer him some look-the-other-way money you'll get in easily enough. Swacky's no great believer in regulations, either. When you've seen what's there and got some pictures, if you like to come back and see me I'll tell you what I can about it – or at least where to go to find out.'

Eglinton was gone for about an hour. It was dusk when the reporter came back, that misty dusk with a remembrance of winter chill in it and which augured a fine spring day on the morrow and the young man was glad to warm himself by Henderson's fire. He said: 'I saw it all and got some pictures of it – but I can't make head nor tail of it. It's impressive all right, but what does it mean?'

'How many of your readers are likely to be archaeologists?'

'None, I should think,' Eglinton said.

'Well in that case all they need to be told is that it's there, it's amazing, it's unique – and that some people believe such things are primitive man's impressions of alien visitors from outer space.' And then, for an hour, Henderson trotted out a peculiar mixture of orthodox archaeological theory, but with a topping of the wilder speculations of the Alien Visitors creed. He started with the Peche Merle and the Lascaux caves in southern France – 'drawings made of the animal life of Europe as it then was, thirty thousand to ten thousand years ago' – and moved on to the barrows and cromlechs and stone circles of neolithic Britain. He described most carefully the repeated symbols on the standing stones of northern Scotland, the twin circles or Devil's Spectacles, the lightning, the whale and the serpent. 'Your readers love a mystery,' he said. 'These symbols are mysteries; no-one – well, almost no-one – has ever explained their meaning. And here we have them, hidden underground in a cave which has lain undiscovered for thousands of years: a message left by our earliest post-ice-age ancestors for us to find and understand. But this time they've also left a huge drawing of a man – but what kind of a man? A man with wings and a strange hat. A man who came flying in from space?' He commended the Beaumont theory of the Comet and he lent him a copy, with marked passages, of Von Daniken's effulgences. 'I'd say you've got all the ingredients there of a lovely mystery with enough loose, unexplained ends to get plenty of speculation going.'

Eventually the reporter asked him the question he had been waiting for. 'What do you think, personally, the paintings are about?' he said. 'I mean, do you believe all this about spacemen visiting the earth and starting civilisation off?'

Henderson appeared to ponder for a minute. Then he said: 'It's a sort of hobby-horse of mine, what people will believe and what they won't. I mean, there are millions of people, some of them very well educated, who believe this world was created in six days, about six thousand years ago, aren't there? Others still insist that the earth is flat. Thousands of people think that there is some mysterious force in the Bermudan sea which sucks ships and aeroplanes down to disaster. There is a highly-respected astronomer who thinks that viruses, including the AIDS virus, have dropped on us from Outer Space. More millions of Chinese than I care to think about worship the spirits of their ancestors. Most of Christendom believe in some way or another in a series of events and miracles which are so unlikely that the simple faith of our ancestors in the sanctity of certain stones and the divinity of the sun seems far preferable. There's no limit, is there, to the ability of people to believe anything they want to believe? No matter how strange it is. So a belief in Flying Saucers and visiting spacemen doesn't seem any less likely than any of the others, does it?'

'Er. Er, I suppose not,' said Eglinton and went on his way to write the story which would win him a staff post on one of Britain's biggest daily newspapers.

The headline said: THE GOD UNDER THE EARTH. And, lower down the page: HAVE FLYING SAUCERS LANDED – IN THE SCOTTISH HIGHLANDS? The photographs

Eglinton had taken had printed very well. The twin circles bisected by the zigzag 'lightning' glared like malevolent eyes out of the page. But it was the centre-spread reproduction of the inner cave drawing which really arrested the eye. There, in graceful flowing lines of ochre and black was the startling figure, nine feet high, uncovered by Dr Mould and his assistant – legs astride as if caught by that ancient artist of genius in the act of movement, hands on hips, a male figure of uncompromising masculinity enfolded in what seemed like rudimentary suggestions of angels' wings and with what might have been, and certainly would be claimed to be, a shape like a halo around its mighty head.

Eglinton's story, as re-written, pre-digested, loaded with extra sugar and permitted additives, flavour-enhanced by expert re-write men, went in part like this:

> A mysterious twin-headed comet and a strange drawing of a spaceman from pre-history found in a cave under a Highland hill seem sure to change archaeology's ideas of how civilisation on this earth began.
>
> They reopen the age-old question: were the old pagan gods of our ancestors spacemen from another world who crash-landed here thousands of years ago?
>
> Did our ancestors see the visitors' space craft crashing in flames and draw pictures of it and of a survivor of the wreck on the walls of their cave?
>
> Were the Biblical angels men from another planet?
>
> The answers to these and many more questions which have puzzled men of science for many years may lie beneath a hill in a cave in the Highlands of Scotland.
>
> Today we carry exclusive pictures taken by our reporter, Don Eglinton, of the paintings on the walls of a secret cave at Laidmore in the Northern Highlands. These paintings were made by our remote ancestors as they crouched in the dark and cold in their refuge thousands of years before the birth of Christ.
>
> And the question they pose is: was Von Daniken right and did early man have a close encounter with men from another

world? Are the mysterious double circles, known to archaeologists as 'the Devil's Spectacles', which the cavemen drew on the walls meant to represent the spacemens' flying saucers? And is the zigzag 'lightning' symbol the way these primitive men would represent, in the only way they knew how, the fiery propulsion system of the spaceships' motors? Many experts believe this is a possible interpretation.

But the picture of the giant 'spaceman' is something archaeologists have never seen before. Experts believe he was worshipped as a god by our early ancestors and that he may have come to be identified with another winged figure – a forerunner of Hermes or Mercury, the winged ancient Greek messenger of the gods.

Hermes, also known to the ancient Egyptians as Thoth, appears in nearly every ancient religion, even among peoples who had no links with Greece or Rome or Egypt. The experts see this as further proof that Hermes really existed and that it is not just coincidence that he is often depicted with wings on his heels and wearing a strange hat. Was he, they ask, a portrait of a visiting spaceman from a vastly superior culture and is that 'hat' or halo really a primitive drawing of a transparent space helmet?

Samples of the 'paints' which were used by primitive man to make the pictures and of other objects found in the caves are now being tested by archaeologists to find their exact age. But already this looks like being one of the oldest cave-painting discoveries ever made, perhaps as old, or older even, than the famous paintings in the Lascaux caves in France.

There is no doubt that this remote part of the Scottish Highlands will become a mecca for classical archaeologists as well as for thousands of people who believe in the 'ancient spaceman' theory of civilisation. Local authorities will have to take urgent measures to protect the site.

Eglinton's story, as well as taking up the entire centrefold of the newspaper, was also padded out by several additional features, one of which was a re-hash of the Comyns Beaumont comet theory, combined with some modern orthodox research which supported the idea of a movement of neolithic culture from the north of Britain to the south, and thence to continental Europe instead of the long-held conventional belief of a movement in the opposite direction. In a newspaper which unashamedly played on the impulse of national chauvinism, this was a theory of early culture which suited it admirably. And there was a brief story attributing the discovery to Dr Nathaniel Mould and a quotation from him that it was 'too early to comment' and 'what may turn out to be a discovery of the utmost importance.'

Henderson, in the otherwise empty lunchtime cocktail bar of the Caledonian Hotel, with the newspaper across the counter, clinked celebratory champagne glasses with Simon Briggs and drank to a prosperous future. Simon was displaying an unusual generosity of spirit as well as an unwonted liberality with his wine. 'To you the glory,' he said. 'I must admit now that you've done it, I didn't think it would work. But this is better than anything I hoped for.'

'I hate to have to say this: but the work has only just begun,' Henderson said. 'To make it work we have to keep up the pressure and turn it into a sort of campaign with something new and newsworthy, or at the very least with something said about it, every other week.'

'Surely it'll just keep going on its own, now,' said Simon.

'Not so. Every advertising man knows it: he can produce the cleverest, the gaudiest, the most successful puff in the business, but unless it's repeated and repeated ad nauseam, it won't sell no pertaters. We've got to keep the furnace stoked up until it generates enough heat of its own to keep going – and that means a helluva lot of hard work yet.'

For a while, though, the publicity acquired its own momentum. Several things began happening immediately. Three, then four, then five feature-writers and photographers arrived from two of the more serious Sunday newspapers and a couple of news-agencies and, treading on their heels, a television crew with an outside broadcasting unit in a white van which blazoned its purpose in large letters on its sides and they tried, at first in vain, to gain access to the site. They had been temporarily blocked by urgent telephone calls from Dr Mould which had resulted in an overnight crop of Trespassers Will Be Prosecuted notices planted around the perimeter fence and the reinforcement of Swacky's guardianship in the person of one James McGillivray, who was older, sober and more taciturn than he. Constable McNeill made several appearances in his official Northern Constabulary car and smilingly and stubbornly refused to let anyone through the locked gate. Several times in the twenty-four hours the phalanx of writers and lensmen from Glasgow, Edinburgh and a two-man team from London, sometimes severally, sometimes together, tried the Cnocdruidh defences from several angles but were repulsed. Henderson watched them with amusement from his house until eventually, on Swacky's advice, they came to see him. Of course he could arrange to get them in, he said, but unless they wanted a lot of harassment they would be well advised to repair meanwhile to the Caledonian Hotel bar until the hours of darkness and then to try again in the small dark hours of the morning when McGillivray, the ex-gamekeeper, would be in bed and Swacky would be on the overnight shift.

'And Swacky Ross won't bother you much. In fact if you feel generous enough to put him on your expense accounts he'll show you where to go and probably lend you a ladder. But for Christ's sake leave that bloody broadcasting van out in the street in front of the hotel and then everyone'll think you're tucked up in bed. Coppers watch vehicles in this part of the world and everywhere else as far as I know, not people – it's easier.'

And so it proved. It takes a great deal to push the cork down on an experienced reporter and almost nothing on the face of this earth can solemnise a professional news photographer. But at three o'clock in the morning in the damp underground chill of the Cnocdruidh Caves eight newsmen stood in awe, briefly silenced by the huge silhouette of Hermes, Messenger of the Gods, the Spaceman under the ground, the ancient visitor from another world unimaginably far away, unimaginably alien. In the brilliant light of the torches in that secret spot, even Henderson was deeply impressed and Swacky was stricken with wonderment.

Henderson thought once more: I wonder if something carried from age to age in our genes from that distant savage past guided mine and Alison's hands when we painted this thing. Is it all, entirely, a lie? For the great black and ochre figure, outlined on the smooth rock in the barest economy of line, seen now in the flare of the electric torches of the journalists seemed, somehow . . . animated; it seemed ready to leap outwards from the wall and as you glanced away from it it seemed to move. Undoubtedly it was a combination of this purity of line with which it had been drawn and of a certain inspiration which its authors had felt as they made it, and added to this the ancient and secret environment where it lay – these things combined gave it this numinous presence. Undoubtedly – and yet they, seeing it now, Henderson was finding it difficult to believe that he and Alison had drawn it only a few months ago. There was no doubt that the journalists were impressed too. These were men of a different stamp to Eglinton: they were the products of various universities and at their high schools they had been among the brightest of their year; they were sophisticated men, of catholic education and widely read and informed. And yet they, too, were impressed. The writers among them did not make notes or recordings; there was really nothing to make notes about for it was all very simple. The photographers, though, had a lovely time. Henderson learned that there is apparently nothing more difficult than taking pictures that will mean anything to a newspaper reader of simple line drawings on a rock wall. The problems of lighting, of comparison with familiar objects to demonstrate scale, problems of contrast and colour kept them occupied for nearly two hours until Swacky and Henderson were becoming restive and dawn was beginning to brighten the sky outside after the short May night. 'Not that I think you'd be in much trouble,' Henderson explained to a fat English writer from one of the more intellectually pretentious Sunday newspapers, 'because trespass isn't a crime in Scotland. It's a matter for the civil courts and private prosecution and almost impossible to pursue. And I can't see what other laws you're breaking as long as you don't damage anything. But it would be a bit embarrassing for me if we were caught down here and it would definitely cost Swacky Ross his temporary job . . . so?' The newspapermen were cold and damp anyway and the offer of hot coffee and brandy, of toast and eggs and other delights in Henderson's kitchen had them on the move well before the sun came up and the solemn McGillivray could catch them. (It wasn't going to take the deductive powers of an Einstein to work out, once the pictures and stories had appeared in a series of weekend journals, who had let the journalists into the caves. Swacky was going to lose his job, anyway.)

Over breakfast David Henderson tilled and sowed his ground as thoroughly as he dared. There is, he knew, a perversity in most people whereby if you offer them something free the gift is looked upon with instant suspicion and this applied in double-measure to worldly-wise newspapermen. Even to lead them to the water they so desire to drink is to run the risk of having it treated as poison. And so if he could make these men believe that the ideas he was giving them were, in fact, their own, they would grasp them and speedily forget where they came from. With great circumspection he therefore led them over a long rambling breakfast up some peculiar by-ways of popular archaeological theories and lunacies. But first he gave them a little disquisition on brochs – those curious and unexplained conical forts distributed throughout the Scottish Highlands, whose purpose and whose builders are as yet unknown. He told them about sculptured standing stones which lie in equal profusion throughout the land, and thence to considerations of the lunatic fringes of pre-history: the culture of the Picts, runes, stone-circle telepathy and astronomy, Ley lines, Comyns Beaumont and Immanuel Velikovsky . . . and they all laughed at Von Daniken together. All that the promoters of this archaeological hoax needed after all was publicity, and if this took the form of a sarcastic sneer at the lunatic fringe while it featured the Cnocdruidh discovery, all this was grist to the mill. All Henderson needed to do was to hint at a mystery: that some deity was depicted on the cave walls who was certainly alien to whatever Stone Age culture had been presumed to exist at this time and this far north. And, having planted these seeds, all he had to do was hope that they would germinate, sprout and grow and bear the fruit of tourism. And the result was, indeed, most satisfying.

> ' . . . and, no doubt, those who look for visiting neolithic spacemen under every Silbury Hill or for landing beacons for flying saucers in lines drawn on the Mexican desert, will make a similar interpretation of the Cnocdruidh Hill discoveries . . . ' wrote one respected correspondent in the colour magazine supplement of his Sunday newspaper a week later. But the full-page studies of the great Cnocdruidh figure and of the lightning and twin circles of the outer cave were an arresting sight.

Another of the visiting journalists, the fat one, Henderson remembered, the one who had brandy in his breakfast coffee and a third helping of scrambled eggs and toast, wrote, inter alia:

> 'Serious archaeology may never be able to identify with certainty the giant human figure on the inner cave wall, but what is certain is that there will be some on the fringe – what may be called the lunatic fringe – who will have no difficulty at all in giving this majestic figure an identity. He will be the Man from Mars, or the Creature from Venus, or an Ancient Flying Saucer Captain – whichever takes their fancy.'

Another had written:

> 'Only a detailed assessment of the exciting new discoveries which have been made here will determine how important they are to a re-interpretation of the spread of neolithic culture on mainland Britain. No doubt Dr Mould and his assistants will be expecting to find a great deal more yet.
>
> But one thing is certain: the unique and imposing giant figure of the winged man in the inner cave is bound to fuel the speculations of the lunatic fringe of archaeology – that area where astrology, necromancy, the occult and science-fiction join together in a fantastical hotch-potch. Orthodox archaeology must, though, take some of the blame for this

speculation. Even now, the accepted interpretation of the recurrent theme on Scottish standing stones of the twin circles and zigzag and the beasts and symbols and men portrayed beneath, is that they represent a "hunting scene". Anything less convincing would be hard to find and so, for the want of a sensible analysis of these symbols the more romantic mind will turn inevitably to fantasy . . .'

There was much more in the same vein and it was a well-pleased David Henderson who, on the evening of the day these stories were printed, wrote another of his despatches to Alison Fraser, who was still stubbornly absent hundreds of miles to the south.

Dear Ally,

You'll have seen the Serious Sundays. The Kincardine Cabal, as I've taken to calling myself, Simon, Hugh and Co., were rather taken aback by all the publicity and the snide attitude of the writers until I explained the old music hall troupers' aphorism: it doesn't matter what they're saying about you, dearie, so long as they're saying something.

Swacky, poor bugger, has been kicked out of his job – the only full-time permanent one he's ever had – by the good doctor, for treachery or incompetence, I couldn't quite discover which. The sacking was done at long range, by telephone, through me, and Mould was wild all right, so wild that I couldn't at first make out who or what it was on the telephone; it sounded like an enraged wasp in a bottle. Swacky, though, is bearing up well and he's been celebrating a bit for the last couple of days 'cos the Press Gang have made him quite rich. He could see this regular job, week in, week out, stretching ahead of him forever like a jail sentence. I have another Swacky-ism for you. He confused me no end yesterday by suggesting that he should ask Dr Mould for what I thought were his 'red undies'. Now the good doctor is one of the last people I would suspect of such an exotic tendency and it was quite some time before my startled brain translated this into 'redundancy' – redundancy money. I seem to have talked him out of any such approach.

Which brings me to my last point. Swacky – and the others – keep asking me when you're coming back up again and I'm at a loss to think up any more excuses for you. So maybe you'd better pay us a visit to allay their anxieties for you.

Come to think of it, I wouldn't mind seeing you, too.

HARVEST

CHAPTER NINE

The Kincardine Cabal was in closed session. The problem before them was simple in concept, complex in execution: how best to exploit the publicity which now attended the Cnocdruidh God; how to keep that ferment going and how to turn it into tourist cash. The meeting was taking place in the octagonal glass building attached to David Henderson's house: a baroque conservatory which someone, long ago, had turned into a spectacularly unsuccessful tea-room and which Henderson had turned into an almost equally unsuccessful craft and souvenir shop. There were six present – Simon Briggs, Monty Dickinson, back from Ceylon and looking worried, Hugh Ross, Henderson and Swacky and Cal Jefferson, back from his winter in California. As they talked together they had to raise their voices from time to time as an unseasonal June storm of rain and wind came rolling down from the surrounding hills, thrashing the brilliant sea of golden broom which was now in full flourish everywhere and hammering on the windows.

Sometimes an especially violent gust of wind would wipe the streaming rain clear from the north-facing side of the house for an instant, giving momentary glimpses of the bulk of Cnocdruidh and the grey outcroppings of sheared granite protruding through the luxuriant growth of June, each one sluiced by its little individual cascade of white water. A small flock of sheep was at centre stage of this watery wilderness, their backs turned to the gale, their heads down, waiting patiently for it to pass.

The Squadron Leader attempted a summing up. 'Priority One,' he said, holding up a big hand and pulling down one finger for each point, 'we need a management committee to get things going and we have nominees for that. Priority Two' – down went another finger – 'we've got to raise some money to make a small access road and parking area until such time as the local government authority will take it over and complete a more permanent access. Priority Three: we have to place and man a small information caravan during normal hours which will distribute information leaflets and other publicity . . . ' Henderson found his mind wandering: essential as all these details were, this sort of routine administration was for others to do, he felt. His own priority, as the mess of tools, timber and building materials in the octagon testified, was to enlarge and enhance his souvenir shop and pottery, and he had this well in hand. Simon Briggs was also similarly occupied. Other hoteliers as well as he were beginning to wake up to the possibilities of trade deriving from the Cnocdruidh Caves but Simon, forewarned, was well ahead of the pack. 'A new name and a new image to go with it,' he had told Henderson excitedly before the meeting started. 'We're going to be the Cnocdruidh Hotel as soon as the authorities register the new name. And we're having a new bar called The Cave – overtones of a French wine cellar, if you know what I mean – all stone walls and rough timber and maybe some big prints of the cave paintings on the walls. But tasteful – what I mean, not too touristy, not brash or blatant – and the sort of cuisine you don't get around here at the moment.'

Henderson switched his attention back to Hugh Ross and the others. Monty Dickinson, the landowner, was describing the latest moves in the quiet but ferocious battle which had been joined between his solicitors, supported by the Cabal, and the Ancient Monuments Commission, prodded and manipulated by Dr Mould, who wanted to deny access to everybody except the accredited archaeological team. So far Dr Mould's forces were losing the battle and a compromise had been reluctantly entered into by which visitors would be limited to a wooden platform elevated a few feet above the cave floor with the paintings roped off to protect them from touching hands. The archaeologists were to be allowed a watching brief to ensure no damage or disturbance was done and their continuing explorations and excavations were to receive an undisturbed priority during certain specified hours. 'The Commission and the University are starting work on the platform this week,' Dickinson reported, 'so we should have access for the public in a couple of weeks – but all this is costing me lawyers' time and other expense and you chaps are going to have to pitch in and help me out.' Dickinson was a worry; he was a man with severe ideas of rectitude and what he regarded as fair play and, although he would benefit more quickly than anybody in fees for the use of otherwise unproductive land, yet he nursed an aggrieved feeling that he was being left out of the profit-making. Like most Highland landowners he was always short of money, as the wages of his employees were remorselessly pushed upwards year by year while the Government squeezed him harder and harder for taxes. When the meeting seemed to have reached an impasse on this (Henderson suspected to Monty's secret delight for he had a small boy's pleasure in setting cats among pigeons and then withdrawing to enjoy the subsequent confusion), Cal Jefferson, who had remained uncharacteristically silent throughout, sprawling his huge bulk seemingly over a quarter of the room but remaining so quiet that several times Henderson looked at him curiously to see if he had fallen asleep – Cal suddenly sat bolt upright and said: 'Now look here, you guys, this ain't my country and I'm reluctant to go blundering in here like some boisterous brawling Yank in case you tell me to go mind my own goddam business, but I'll tell you this: you're on to one hell of a good prospect here and I don't mind telling you it's got me pretty excited. Now my old man always told me – and he was a pretty successful entrepreneur – "when you see something good on the market, boy, buy four of them". Well, I believe in this enterprise, and I've some ideas of my own as David, here, knows' – nodding at David Henderson – 'and I'll make you this offer, Monty: whatever you're out of pocket on this, I'll fund it – I can afford it – and once you all get your act together you can refund me whatever you think is fair, once the money starts coming in. Because make no mistake about it, any one of you who gets his act together quickly enough and smartly enough, he's going to make plenty of money, me included.' And that, apart from some thankyous and congratulations all round, took the wind out of everybody's sails and wrapped the meeting up nicely. And when the last one of them had made his dash through the sluicing rain to his vehicle, Cal put a big bear arm on Henderson's shoulder and roared with merriment. 'See those turkeys,' he gasped, 'they were all settling down to have a good old committee meeting which would have kept you out of your bed until after midnight and they would have decided absolutely nothing. And that jive-ass Dickinson, he can't make up his mind whether to take the money or whether to be a gent and decline. Well that's his problem. All we have to do is make sure this little gold mine starts producing the goods.'

Within a week a lot had happened: Dr Mould came storming up to the site in a curious mixture of rage, despair and helplessness. 'If only,' he complained, 'we had been able to keep it quiet for a year or so, we could have completed our study without interference and got out a report which would have squashed all these silly and ignorant stories. Gods, spacemen and flying saucers . . . ' He waved his little plump hands in the air in uncoordinated gestures of irritation. 'Such nonsense, such bloody silly nonsense – and they've got my name associated with it. D'you know, I'm having to do something I've never done before and bring out a preliminary report before we've half-examined the evidence. But if I don't bring out something immediately all my colleagues will think I've gone mad. And now, I've no doubt, all those camp-followers of archaeology, everyone who's read a journalist's book on the subject, will come flocking up here to goggle and stare and make wild and ignorant speculations about what should be a serious and sober academic study.'

'You should feel flattered that they're all so interested.'

'Flattered? Flattered! It is all a terrible, terrible mess and I hold you, Mr Henderson, largely responsible.'

'Me? What am I supposed to have done?'

'I hear stories,' the doctor said. 'You're a man who has some education' (Oh, thank you very much, thought Henderson) 'and you must know that all this comet-and-spaceman stuff is nonsense. You could have told those damned reporters as much instead of encouraging them.' And he went on his way muttering something which sounded like 'treachery'.

But during his brief stormy visit Dr Mould established his assistant, Stephen Ryle, as archaeologist-in-residence and, being young and not a little ingenuous, he was far less intractable than Dr Mould to deal with. Not a move occurred, however, but Ryle wrote it down in a little notebook he carried everywhere and reported almost daily to his master. It proved possible, however, to get enough cooperation from Ryle to install without much argument the platforms in the Caves for the public to walk on, to place rope barriers along the sides, to remove most carefully the turf and soil from the entrance to the Caves and erect broad stout wooden steps down into the interior. A small portable generator had been housed in a little hut and wires and lights were run from it so that the Caves were now brilliantly illuminated. All this had cost quite unimportant amounts of money which it had been possible to raise from locally interested parties; the big expense would be in levelling a car park and making an all-weather access road into the site and Hugh Ross's Management Committee was happily engaged in a long bureaucratic wrangle with local government authorities and various development agencies, official and unofficial, in an attempt to get them to pay for this. Henderson observed, not for the first time, that man was a very strange animal indeed and seemed always to be at his happiest making simple things very complex and then unravelling them into simple things again. Eventually, he knew, the road would be built and the car park would be levelled by a small group of men with shovels, lorries and a road roller but before that happened an immense amount of intricate legal, financial and political dickering would take place involving perhaps a hundred people not one of whom would have known how to drive a road roller and covering enough paper with small black marks to bury Cnocdruidh entirely several inches deep.

'. . . radiocarbon-dating of some of the paint substances from the Cnocdruidh Cave walls has established that the paintings are a great deal older than was first supposed, placing them in the fourth millennium B.C. or about 5,800 to 6,000 years ago. This pre-dates by more than 1,000 years any other evidence so far discovered of settled habitation on the Scottish mainland . . .

'. . . the twin-circles and zigzag motif in the outer cave – a design until now thought to be of Pictish origin, will undoubtedly give rise to much speculation . . .

'. . . the paint substances themselves, which have been preserved remarkably well, seem from the necessarily small amounts we were able to remove without damaging the designs to have been a mixture of charcoal and grease, animal blood and other substances which it has not been possible, at this stage, to identify . . .'

Dr Mould's privately-circulated preliminary report to his academic colleagues, sent to Henderson by Alison Fraser, was a model of equivocation, bristling with whereases, ifs, and necessarily incompletes. He was a little brisker, though, when he moved on to the more familiar ground of the figures themselves and the purpose of the Caves.

'Refuge or temple (he wrote); it seems impossible at this early stage to dismiss either theory. There is, so far, no evidence of a hearth and a noticeable paucity of tools, pottery or midden materials which one would expect to find in some profusion were the caves to have been used for long periods of habitation. But there is much excavation yet to be done and if this can be accomplished without too much damage being done to the site by the premature opening of it to the public, there may well be many surprises and much important new information yet to come from what, it is already apparent, is a discovery of major importance to the archaeology of neolithic Britain.'

Alison had underlined the 'many surprises' phrase and written in the margin 'and how!' in red ink. (In her accompanying letter she said it would be very unwise for her to be seen around the site for a while yet. Stephen Ryle knew her well and was not to be dismissed as an ingenu because of his somewhat batty appearance: he was a shrewd fellow in many ways who might start putting two and two together and making dangerous arithmetic. It would only need someone local to tell him she'd spent many weeks in the area only a year previously to start him wondering about the coincidence of her being on the doorstep of a major archaeological discovery. 'But don't doubt that I want to see you all badly and we'll be getting together soon,' she wrote. David Henderson could have wished that she had written the simple 'you' instead of 'you all' but he preferred to put the best gloss he could on it.)

It was late June now, and through the glass of the octagonal room the gold of the broom was now half spent and fading to brass, but other colours – grey of whinstone and granite and the profusion of those muted flower colours of nature rather than of a cultivated garden: white with a dusting of pink, blue with a shading of violet – were taking over the slopes of Cnocdruidh. And, growing more numerous every day, among that wilderness moved the violent colouration of city man in his nylon anoraks, his aniline-dyed and strident holiday clothing, exotic and disturbing in this muted landscape. His harsh cries overlaid the familiar and ancient noise of curlew and water rushing through rocks, the hiss of wind in birch thickets and deer grass. For the first tributary trickle of the curious, breaking aside from the arterial flood, was eddying into Kincardine and finding its way to the Cnocdruidh site, not yet officially open. To Henderson's great satisfaction and profit most of them were coming to the octagonal room for refreshments and information and many paused also to buy the craft goods on display there. Already Simon Briggs's hotel was showing a twenty per cent improvement on the previous year's disastrous business slump and this foretaste of what was to come smoothed the worry on his brow and put a spring in his step which Henderson had not seen for many a year.

'Have you noticed,' Simon said, 'how many of these people are, what I mean, Flat Earthers? I listen to them in the bar and they're definitely of a type.' Flat Earthers in Simon's lexicography embraced a range of people, mostly young, who, without a very sound scholastic basis, had set themselves against all forms of orthodoxy but who had, sadly, merely replaced them with an orthodoxy of their own within which they moved, believing themselves freed. Simon's Flat Earthers believed in Ley Line magic, in whole foods, holistic medicine and the value of herbs and meditation, in yoga and ancient astronauts. There was a prevailing type among them, marked by a similarity in dress and even in a leanness of figure, which it was quite possible to identify with a high degree of accuracy after a while. They were mostly youngish or on the younger side of middle age; often they were vegetarian, or vegetarian-inclined and many of the men were bearded and wore jeans and training shoes and a high proportion of the women had long straight hair, wore loose dresses and, if they had babies, usually made a point of breast-feeding them in public, no matter how inconvenient this might be. Their vocabulary tended to be spotted with words such as 'angst' and 'catharsis' and there were phrases culled from the jargon of sociology which had very little meaning. Stockhausen tended to be admired, Klee found too sentimental. Henderson liked them for they were gentle people, atheists mostly, looking for a new religion and ritual to illuminate their lives and he found them a lot less lunatic than many a stockbroker or town councillor he had known. They insisted on scientific proof for all the things they did not want to believe but embraced with childlike and engaging innocence new fads of belief from the mysteries of bending spoons and mending watches by thinking at them, to the uses of acupuncture in virus-carried diseases and strange theories of man being raised from the ape by wise and gentle beings from beyond the stars. Simon seemed to despise them, but he appreciated the trade.

David Henderson frequently found himself in conversation with groups of these visitors when they stopped at his house for directions to Cnocdruidh. They were open, friendly and intelligent and ready to share their preoccupations as if they had known him intimately for a long time instead of for a few minutes. He found their openness an astonishing change from the attitude of his fellow Highlanders, who were usually very willing to talk but on an entirely acquisitive basis: they would tell you nothing which you wanted to know while expertly preparing the ground for you to make damaging indiscretions. Like country people everywhere they were disarmingly expert at this. But these visitors, when they wanted to know something, would simply ask – which was anathema to a Highlander. And they volunteered, at no price of exchange, information about themselves which many a neighbouring Highlander, or even a normally prudent person, would not have disclosed easily even to his family. While Henderson or Swacky were showing them the path to the caves they would, with no prompting at all, go into details of their age and marital status, the predilections of their wives and their children, their own incomes and status at work and their hopes for their future and that of their country with frequent asides on their moral and political beliefs. Swacky was taken aback, confounded and awash in puzzlement. After one particularly revealing session in which he had been made party to family problems and ambitions which he would not, personally, have disclosed to a priest in a confessional, he said to Henderson, producing one of his memorable phrases – 'Man, man, that cratur was bletherin' like a book.'

Most encouragingly, though, the lack of any analytical quality in their thinking once these quite well-educated people were confronted with the Cnocdruidh Caves' marvels filled Henderson with joy and optimism for the future of the project. Ten minutes in that awesome place and, without further question, they dumped their favourite preconceptions on it – those which they had travelled north to confirm. Henderson, in optimistic vein, had predicted this very reaction to the Kincardine Cabal when the projected 'seeding' of the Caves was still in utero, but he had not expected to succeed so well and so easily and it came as a constant surprise and delight to see intelligent people deluding themselves with such alacrity. 'It's going to be the easiest archaeological rip-off in history,' he reported to the others. 'We're off and running because we're preaching to the already-converted. And there's nothing easier than that.'

This optimism was flawed for David Henderson by one factor which was increasingly in his thoughts: the long absence of Alison. He knew her reasons for staying away were good and that it would be irresponsible madness to jeopardise the project by her premature arrival. But, surely, a clandestine visit? If she really wanted to, would that be so difficult? Those conspiratorial weeks together while they seeded the Caves had meant, he realised now, much more to him than he had realised at the time. He had a recurrent fancy that, on the brightest of days, some giant hand was on some celestial rheostat turning down the light of the sun a notch or two, stealing the colour out of the landscape and turning it grey. Alison had made her helpless commitment to him when she was a teenager, a child, and he knew that if he now wanted to prove their present relationship it was he who had to speak. But should he risk the present, such as it was, by gambling on the future? She would not laugh at him – he knew that – but she might be astonished, and appalled. And that thought was like a fist clenching inside him, spreading paralysis like an actual physical pain. He hoped it would go away – and prayed that it wouldn't.

CHAPTER TEN

The little green mini-bus with the linked twin circles of the 'spectacles' bisected by zigzag lightning painted vividly on its sides came rapidly up the single-track road and jounced to a halt outside Henderson's front door: out came the gigantic figure of Cal Jefferson. He reached back inside and held a large poster in front of Henderson's face.

> YOU HAVE HEARD OF THE HIGHLAND WHISKY TRAIL, THE TRAILS OF THE BROCHS AND THE ILL-FATED LOCH NESS MONSTER TRAIL. NOW TAKE THE COMET TRAIL THROUGH PREHISTORIC SCOTLAND TO THE MYSTERIOUS CAVES OF THE SPACE GOD!

The poster screamed its message in four vibrant colours and was adorned with a rudimentary map and outlines of the cave figures.

'Well, what d'you think of it? Neat, eh?'

David Henderson said: 'Christ.'

'Just bought another six of these things,' Cal said, patting the bus with a mighty fist. 'Twelve seats in each one and we're gonna get asses on each seat at fifty pounds each day seven days a week. Each one of these little beauties is gonna earn me four thousand pounds a week – not to mention concessions from the places we stop at on the way. Neat.'

Neat, all right, thought Henderson, making a rapid calculation. Cal was going to make as much in a week as he made in a good full year. That's what capital, energy and an almost total lack of inhibition could do for you. Cal came inside and expounded his operation. The idea had sprung, as he readily gave credit, from four previous schemes, three of which were doing well: the Whisky Trail, the Broch Trail, the Burns Heritage Trail and the Loch Ness Monster Trail. The Whisky Trail, with suitable stops for highly-intoxicating lunches and dinners, toured the famous Highland malt distilleries with sensible descriptions of how Scotch was made, bottled and blended. The Broch Trail, which had provided Cal with his idea, was a similar but much more sober tour of a selection of those hundreds of mysterious pre-Pictish stone towers found on the sea-boards of Caithness, Sutherland, Ross and Inverness, mostly now mere stubs left by generations of stone-robbers who had dismantled them – once the danger of seafaring marauders had passed – to build their cottages. The Burns Heritage Trail took you around the areas of the boozy bard's carousings and romances. But Cal's trail was altogether more ambitious. 'Jefferson's Fourth Law of Entrepreneurship,' he had explained, 'doesn't go for chancy things like new inventions and fresh ideas. Those are for guys who want to gamble with their cash. Jefferson's law says take someone else's idea, once it's been tried and proved, and then do it better and swamp the other bastard.' You would book with Cal for one-to-four-day tours by mini-bus taking in the mysterious standing stones of prehistoric Scotland – sculptured monoliths like the Golspie Stone and vast circles like those at Stenness – with visits to those strange underground houses found in great numbers throughout Highland and Lowland areas and which included Skara Brae on Orkney Island, the most complete and the most famous of them all. You ended, climactically, at the Caves of the Space God, the Cnocdruidh Man. You went everywhere by courtesy of Cal Jefferson. You would travel in his buses, stay, on the more expensive tours, at the hotels which paid him off best, read the literature sold to you and start and end at the hotel which he had converted from a vast old barn less than a mile from the Cave site.

While the Cave 'discovery' was still in the melting pot Cal, as he had intimated to Henderson, had picked up the barns for a couple of thousand pounds. And while, to use Cal's colourful phrase, others would have been 'drag-assing around' with architects, bank managers and assorted government officials and planning officers, he already had the diggers and cement mixers in there. Cal provided an object lesson in how to light the wick under a local bureaucracy which had grown so arthritic in its joints that it could take a man a year to instal a flush lavatory in an old cottage. He bullied the local council's planning officer so consistently and unmercifully that the man was delighted to give in, recommend his plans and grant a building warrant just so that he wouldn't have the fellow breathing down his neck from the time his office opened in the morning until he escaped from it at night. What normally took a year of nit-picking obstructionism had been accomplished in two months, and still Cal had fumed at the delay.

'I used to wonder why things never got done in Britain,' he said, 'why it was we always beat you to the punch even when the ideas came from here – until I met your City Hall officials. If they were put there, once, to help they've sure as hell long forgotten it – and the worst of them are the ones who are supposed to be stimulating business by awarding government grants and loans. Christ, man, they were trying to offer me money at rates of usury which would have made Shylock blush.' One memorable day when there were half a dozen of them standing around on his site, each with a different coloured form and with different helpful advice, he summarily ordered them all off the premises and told them that the best contribution they could make to the success of his enterprise was to 'clear the hell out' and let him get on with it. His tornado-like approach to bureaucracy worked, though, and the sound of digging and hammering was echoing across the valley while Dr Mould and his assistant were making their first assault on the virginity of the Cnocdruidh Caves.

When he had finished admiring Cal's all-or-nothing plunge

into the enterprise, Henderson was curious. 'Why did you go for this approach in particular?' he asked.

'How d'you mean?' Cal said.

'Well. As I see it there're two roads to go down on this. There's the idea of the Ancient Astronaut – the Spaceman who made a stopover on Earth and got his face and his saucer portrayed on the cave walls: the Von Daniken theory. And there's the comet hitting the Earth and destroying a northern civilisation and getting that event, circles-and-lightning, splashed all over cave walls and standing stones – the Beaumont theory. Why go for both? I thought you'd go for the Spaceman alone.'

'I won't deny I was tempted,' Cal said. 'But I applied the Cal Jefferson Rule of Business Number One. Which is: go where the money is. Dead simple. You see, Dave, the Ancient Astronauters are the lunatic fringe of the archaeological world. Have you had a good look at them lately? Beards and boobs, man. Granny dresses and old campers, high brows and short pockets and lots of them on Grass and wholefoods. A nice crowd. I like them. But I don't see them propping up the bar in the Cnocdruidh Lodge, do you? But your comet enthusiasts – you don't have to be a lunatic to believe that. A bit of wishful thinking, maybe. A bit of childlike wonderment and not too much heavy reading. The sort of guys who used to come and gawp at Loch Ness and get into half-serious arguments in the bars around Inverness . . . You know: 'There might just be something there, it's just possible' – that sort of guy. They're genuine tourists, genuine rubber-neckers. They've got cars and money and paid holidays. It's their asses I want on my buses and bar stools. You too, if you know what's good for you.'

For Cal Jefferson this enterprise seemed to be the purpose for which he had prepared himself, from his origins on the arid Kansas farm, about which – reflecting a current American fad for discussing one's roots and origins – he was eager to tell anyone who was interested. This growing period took him through the various disciplines of the United States Marine Corps, in which he had seen some hard action in Korea, through engineering college and the rigours, disasters and successes of American entrepreneurship, first in the mid-West, then in

California and now in the northern Highlands from which his ancestors may have come. He had toughened mentally and physically along the way but despite his fifty-six years he was markedly boyish and enthusiastic, given to flights of fancy and ardour, and full of excitements and mischief to a measure which would have seemed ridiculous in a European. This enterprise had just the blend of larceny and skullduggery which appealed to his sense of humour.

He saw in one flash of inspiration exactly how to exploit the Cnocdruidh discovery, much as a musician is said to see a concerto or a sonata, overture, fugue and scherzo, in a single moment in its complete and integrated whole. He moved into action with characteristic panache, so smoothly that you could not have heard the meshing of the gears and cogs, and he dragged others along with him on the wave of energy he created. But he also had that supreme ingredient of the opportunist entrepreneur: financial resources available at once and in sufficient quantity to enable him to ignore the banks and other institutional money-lenders. He could do what he wanted, when he wanted, with only the local bureaucracy to impede him and long ago he had analysed the workings of such bureaucracies very thoroughly. 'You don't go out and try to fight City Hall,' he said. 'They love that. They get all their kicks out of squashing any new ideas and then hiding behind a book of rules with so many ambivalencies in it that only the lawyers can get rich if you try to challenge it. No. You just campaign in such a way that they're denied this enjoyment and you begin to make the inhabitants of those offices tired of life.' And if they still withstood him he just went out and bribed someone who controlled them. And when Simon and Henderson looked shocked and incredulous at this he patiently explained to them what he called 'Jefferson's Third Law of Corruption'. 'It goes roughly like this: in any political or business deal worth more than, say, fifty thousand bucks – the threshold varies with inflation and relative affluence, so in the Kenyan Mara it might be four oxen and a bucket of blood – someone who is in a position to expedite or to sit on the deal is on the take: not sometimes, not usually, not ninety per cent of the time – but *always*.' And when Simon, not wanting to believe this, asked if he meant local government finance directors and chairmen of committees, those formal and sober-suited planning officers, directors of social welfare, chief engineers and architects, Cal regarded him with a bland and amused eye. 'And it's you who accuse us Yanks of romantic idealism!' he said. 'Yeah, Simon, one or other of them in every deal worth more than a few thousand is on the take. Every time. When one of them gets into the newspapers, as they do from time to time, it's only because that one hasn't been playing the rules of this game and paying off his buddies; he's got too greedy or too stupid. And human nature is no damn different in Albuquerque or Auchtermuchty. The Greed Factor don't change, whether it comes in the form of an invitation to dinner, a crack at your wife – if she's pretty enough – a crate of Malt, a holiday in Malta for two or a question which a couple of elected councillors forget to ask. There are dozens of different ways of bribing someone without actually dumping a bagful of money on their front steps. Show me a real poor elected or appointed official, and if you can find one – which I strongly doubt – I'll show you an ass-hole.'

He was a bloody old likeable pirate, Henderson decided, needing only the cutlass in his hand and the rag around his head to be absolutely and unmistakably in the picture. His total lack of inhibition in the uses of publicity took one's breath away. Cal did not believe in the Outright Lie: he liked his assertions to have at least some basis in fact, but provided the subsequent exaggerations stayed within the law and attracted the maximum business he did not lay down any further guidelines or limitations. 'Like modern poetry,' he said with a twinkle in his eye. 'All metaphor and far-fetched conceits – the truth through hyperbole – and not a lot of rules about style. Impressionistic – know what I mean, Simon?'

The result was a campaign so highly-coloured it could make you wince. But it was already bringing the visitors tumbling over themselves to stay at Cal's Barn and now they would be trundling around the countryside in his mini-buses in ever-increasing numbers, acquiring a strangely distorted view of

Scotland's early and prehistoric past. The long bar, adapted from what had once been the milking parlour of the barn was itself one of those strange melanges of fact, fancy, the artistically tasteful and the downright vulgar. The old flagstone floor had been left much the way it had always been but now, instead of cows standing in patient rows, the patrons stood there unconscious of the strange fact that as they leant on Cal's bar they were standing in much the same attitudes as the past generations of Blossoms, Belles and Dandelions, elbows on the bar, buttocks out-thrust, mooing gently to each other in a contented haze. One wall of this long room had been allowed to remain as it had been built out of rubble masonry, cleaned up and re-pointed. And on its antique surface Cal had had painted a colossal fresco of the symbols on the Cnocdruidh Cave walls and the room was dominated by the lightning-and-spectacles and the huge enigmatic figure of the Cnocdruidh God-Under-The-Ground. 'Hasn't really changed its function much at all,' Cal said to Henderson in a stage whisper on one of his neighbourly visits. 'It's still a milking parlour, in a way.'

On his proposals for the further exploitation of the Cnocdruidh Caves even Cal Jefferson had found his more imaginative ideas blocked by a solid rock of resistance which he could not yet hew a way through. The Ancient Monuments Commission, to which Monty Dickinson had handed over day-to-day control of the site for a sum which amounted to a hundred years of sheep-pasturing, would not, despite his best efforts, allow Cal to instal son-et-lumière equipment below ground, or anywhere within the immediate vicinity. Perhaps later, they said, when the Caves were fully explored, but it would be too damaging and interruptive at this early stage to sling wires and lights and screens and all the rest of the equipment needed for this enterprise. So Cal, with a scarcely perceptible break in his stride, prepared a son-et-lumière of his own – a videofilm of the Comet theory, ending with highlights of the Cave paintings, shown twice daily in the reception area of the hotel where once the sheep had been gathered in the late spring for shearing. 'Not too much change of function there, either,' he whispered to Henderson one day as the latest busload of tourists milled confusedly about in the big room looking for friends, luggage, seats, picture postcards and children and keeping up what from a distance sounded like a continuous worried bleating sound.

Cal's film owed little to orthodox archaeological thought but a great deal to Hollywood and Madison Avenue. It began with a close-up, filling the screen, of the twin circles-and-lightning symbol from one of the hundreds of pre-Christian sculptured monoliths of northern Scotland and a commentator's voice began expounding a curious amalgam of the classical interpretation of these symbols mingled with some of the arcane theories which had grown up around them. 'Flying saucers or the head of a double-comet?' the voice said. 'Is this a message left to us by our terrified forefathers of thousands of years ago as they witnessed an event which was to shatter and change their world completely and forever?' And as the camera moved from symbol to symbol down the monolith, the voice read off their supposed zodiacal resemblances to Aquarius the Water carrier, Aries the Ram, Cetus the Whale, the inverted moon symbol (indicating a deluge) and finally the mounted fleeing figures surrounded by their frieze of animals. 'The same scene with scarcely a variation is etched into giant granite monoliths found in their hundreds throughout the north and west of Scotland,' intoned the commentator. 'Only one explanation of their purpose has ever made convincing sense and that is that these stones record some great and all-encompassing event which etched itself into the race-memory of these people just as they themselves etched it into the stone. Classical archaeologists say these figures depict a hunting scene – but we cannot imagine a hunting scene which took place in identical style from one seaboard to the other over an area of thousands of square miles of trackless wilderness, all at one time and all in the same manner. For these sculptured stones were not the result of idle activity done in a careless moment; this tremendous labour was done in a harsh land, in conditions of desperate necessity, in the midst of a harsh environment where life was hardly won and sustained. Why would a primitive people expend such effort and time which could otherwise have been spent in those pursuits which were urgently necessary for survival in a land of cold and storm and frost, unless these symbols were of such paramount importance that survival itself took second place? Follow the trail with us and we believe we can show you the astonishing answer.'

Mystery – evidence – denouement, Henderson had to agree that Cal had done the thing terribly well. For now, as the film ran on in a strange pastiche of the factual and the fanciful, a story unfolded of a race of people confronted by cataclysm or a visitation of such moment that they had bent every effort towards recording it for a warning or for worship. Remorselessly, step by step, through a trail of monoliths and weems, cromlechs, stone circles and buried underground dwellings and tumuli the journey led to the Cnocdruidh Caves where, alongside the twin-circle symbols appeared the winged and helmeted giant figure of the man-god. 'Was this the visitor, possessor of unimagined powers, come from beyond the stars, from whom our ancestors fled in awe and terror? And was it his arrival in brightness and flame, surrounded by lightnings and huge energies, which sent them cowering underground to record in the only way they knew how, that awful arrival?

'And has he survived down the waste of years as Mercury, winged messenger of the gods, Hermes, the mystic figure worshipped by Britons and Romans alike, or Lucifer, the Dark One, the Fallen Angel of the Bible cast down by Heaven in flood and ruin?'

Despite what he knew, David Henderson was himself impressed more than he would have believed possible. Was there something in it, after all, he wondered? Then he cleared the absurd idea from his mind. There is, he reasoned, a need in all of us for ritual and worship arising from who knows what flaws and incompletenesses in our psyche, but to go out and deliberately create a God and then to start believing in it was too ridiculous to contemplate. And yet, and yet . . .

And then Cal, speaking softly in his ear, effectively dispelled that illusion in a moment. 'Just see those dude-asses lapping it all up,' he murmured, indicating his rapt customers. 'I reckon I could sell 'em grandstand tickets for the Second Coming if I hit them with it right now.'

Simon Briggs was showing increasing signs of restiveness, always much more evident when he had been visiting Cal Jefferson's place. Henderson believed the basis of this malaise was jealousy but couldn't quite understand why. But one night, not long after Cal had introduced his new mini-bus fleet and Henderson and Simon had been entertained by the big American to dinner, Simon spoke out.

All through the evening he had been less than whole-hearted in his praise of Cal's expanding enterprise and he had kept dropping little waspish remarks which Cal appeared not to notice but Henderson, knowing him better, was sure that he did. The two hoteliers were such disparate personalities that harmony between them was impossible. Now, as they walked back down the road and halted at Simon's car and Henderson waited for him to get in it and drive away, his anxieties were confirmed.

'Who is this fellow Jefferson anyway?' Simon said. 'He's only been here, what I mean, five minutes and he seems to be taking over the entire tourist business – or intending to – in the whole area.'

'Hell, Simon, you're doing all right, aren't you? Surely there's enough here for everybody.'

'And you seem to be spending a hell of a lot of time with him. What I mean – you used to be over at my place every other day and this is the first time I've had a chance to speak to you for nearly a fortnight. Dropping all your old friends for this Yank, are you? Off with the old – on with the new?'

Henderson thought: he makes us sound like lovers. I've grown accustomed to his charms. All of a sudden I've become aware of the fading bloom on the cheek, the elastic lightsome step which is becoming a tired shuffle, the bright laughing greeting, the giggles and thrills of sharing our hopes and fears all fading to a weary routine and a sham. Bloody hell, he cursed silently, I've been through all this before with a woman; God save me from having to endure it with Simon. He was getting tired of these tantrums, he was middle-aged, it was a hell of a job keeping the complicated little net of the Cnocdruidh fraud mended and intact and he didn't want to have to make all those little extra adjustments and allowances and charitable forgivenesses for anyone, least of all for the sort of old woman Simon was developing into.

There was danger, too, in all this xenophobia and jealousy of Simon's. Hell, he thought sardonically, hath no fury like that of a paranoid hotelier scorned. What if he got so peevish and jealous that he ditched the lot of them to get some muddled revenge? This sort of self-flagellation was something which arrogant and unstable natures like Simon's were perfectly capable of. And so, hating the task while he yet did it, he began to make the emollient adjustments necessary to pacify him.

'Don't you worry about the Cals of this world, Simon,' he said. 'Think of them as buccaneers. They love to challenge the system and take on all comers – to buck it and win. We're not like that. The Cals make a lot of waves, a lot of turmoil and people like you and me can do very well in the froth they generate. But his way of going about things isn't your way – or mine – and he's not going to tread on your toes, Simon. He'll be away off in the distance, on the skyline of the next hill, roaring and waving his arms about and making a hell of a din while you're quietly consolidating your gains.' (Or, more likely, he thought, up to your armpits in tickle-points of legal niceties and getting absolutely nowhere, you old stick-in-the-mud.)

Eventually, grumbling, Simon allowed himself to be mollified but Henderson realised that like a wearied suitor who has lost all taste for the chase he would have to pursue this courtship no matter how much he detested it.

A pettish, disprized Simon would be a continuing danger to them all and threaten all their hopes.

CHAPTER ELEVEN

Dear Mr Jefferson,

I don't know whether you realise it, but the fame of the Caves of Cnocdruidh at Kincardine and of your Comet/Flying Saucer Trail has spread as far as Canada and I was reading about it in my Toronto Star only yesterday. There are several things about the newspaper story, though, which I find real puzzling.

First, I had better introduce myself. I was born in the village of Kincardine sixty-three years ago and was brought out here by my parents when I was fifteen. I have not been back since that day we left forty-eight years ago. But I have the clearest memories of my boyhood there and I believe I could still identify every rock and stream in the area for many miles around which my friend Lachie Stewart and I explored as 'loons' during the long summer holidays. Lachie, I believe, went to Australia and I haven't heard of or from him in many a day. But what I am writing to you about, sir, is that I am virtually certain that the Cnocdruidh Caves mentioned in the newspaper story must be the very same caves which Lachie and I discovered as boys and used as our lair, or den. As loons we kept it a deadly secret and made vows to tell no other person about them, in the way lads will. I remember well that Lachie, who was something of a fan of the red Indians and fancied himself as an Apache, made the two of us swear a 'blood oath' which involved the two of us making scratches on our arms and mixing our blood. We then swore a terrible oath, binding us forever not to reveal the secret of the caves and I believe I would not do so even now if you hadn't discovered them for yourselves.

What is puzzling me a great deal and why I am writing to you, sir, is that when we used to play down in the caves during those summers of long ago there were certainly no paintings on the walls, no Space God, and no twin-circles, lightning or any other symbols. Someone must have put them there since, so they can't be more than forty-eight years old, never mind 6,000. I think you ought to be made aware of what seems to be a hoax before you sink any more money into it.

Now I am planning my first visit back to the Old Country since I first emigrated and I expect to visit Kincardine in a few weeks' time. I will call on you then, if I may, and propose to keep quiet about the caves until then in case there is some chance of a mistake. Perhaps there are two sites – though I really doubt it profoundly because we, Lachie and me, explored every inch of that hill, above and below ground. But I will only know for absolute certain once I see them again for myself. I do hope for all your sakes that there are other caves which we did not discover but I really don't think this is possible. I look forward to meeting you later this month.

The letter was signed: 'Andrew Ross'. There was a postscript: 'One reason why the existence of the caves may have been forgotten or have lain unsuspected all these years is that the day before I was to go to Canada with my parents, Lachie and me rolled a great big boulder over the entrance so that our secret would be safe. I have a memory of us leaving certain things down there but this is a little vague and I can't be precise about it.'

The Squadron Leader read these last few words to his audience, put the letter down on the table, took off his reading glasses slowly and replaced them carefully in his spectacles case and put it in his pocket. He looked at the others in turn: Cal Jefferson, Simon Briggs and David Henderson. He said: 'I've been afraid of something like this from the very beginning. Now, what do we do? Try to brazen it out? Or call the whole thing off and make a clean breast of it?' And he looked especially hard and sternly at Henderson, as at a ringleader whose leadership had failed and was liable to summary justice. But it was Cal who raised a large hand, palm flat towards the Squadron Leader in the universal gesture: Wait. Hold on. Peace. 'Forget any ideas like that,' he said. 'I've got a two hundred thousand dollar investment riding on this and I don't give up that kind of money quite so easy. We can keep this guy quiet if we go about it the right way . . . now don't look at me that way, Briggs, I'm not talking about fitting him with concrete boots and sinking him in the Loch. I'm well aware this ain't Chicago circa 1918. There are plenty of other ways. We can quite probably simply talk him out of it, or convince him he's mistaken, or pay him off, or frighten the bejasus out of him. Lots of ways short of concrete footwear, Simon.'

Cal's audience, though, was less than convinced by his cheerful ebullience. 'It's damned serious,' gloomed Simon, refusing to be in the least bit comforted. 'What I mean – if this feller Andrew Ross gets talking to the newspapers . . . What then? Then the stuff will really hit the fan, won't it? What I mean – I've spent money I haven't got, not just promoting the Caves but on new chalets, a totally refurbished dining room, a bloody craft shop and Pizza Parlour – the lot. This bloke's *got* to keep his mouth shut or the bank'll put the boot right in and I'll be right out.' Henderson noted with concern that he had begun pulling at his left ear lobe again and snuffling between sentences – always a bad sign.

'Brace up, Briggs,' the Squadron Leader said. 'It's the same, more or less, for all of us . . . even me.' The others stared at him and he looked, for a moment, strangely shy. Henderson began, at last, to find himself really liking him for the first time. 'I know I said at the beginning that I'd go along with the, er, deception so long as it didn't hurt anybody, but that I wouldn't profit by it. But, well, it seemed such a capital idea once I got used to it, and especially after the railways and the other people had, so to speak, kicked us in the teeth and treated us with such contempt and lied to us. And, well, hang it, I decided to get in on it too in a smallish way. We've done up a part of the old house for en-famille dinners – venison and grouse and fine wines and the like – and spent rather more than we can afford. We were planning to open next week and I was going to invite all of you along for a sort of inaugural dinner. So I'm in this up to the neck, too.'

Henderson was surprised – and delighted – and chastened. It heightened his concern that the whole thing could go awry for he knew that if this happened the whole blame would be his. Without him there would have been no painted caves, no re-birth of business and hope in the area: no glittering prize to be snatched away at the very last moment by a loud-mouthed North American expatriate. He realised at that instant that he could not allow this to happen, that he would not allow this to happen, that he would work harder and more cunningly than he had ever worked in his life to make sure that these people who had followed his lead and had trusted his judgement would not lose everything because of any failure which he could do something about. He thanked his usual good luck for placing Cal Jefferson on the scene with his massive self-confidence and his irrepressible optimism.

He said: 'The obvious thing to do, before we even think about defeat, is to write to this Ross character. It's going to take a bit of tact, a bit of subtlety. I'm not up to it on my own, but let me draft a letter to him and then we'll all get together and sub-edit it. Another thing to do is to get a bit of research going on him. He's almost one of your contemporaries, Hugh, isn't he? And there must be plenty of other people around here – where they all seem to live to about ninety anyway – who still remember him and – who knows? – we may find something useful – '

'Yeah. Get the dirt on the bastard,' said Cal with a huge theatrical leer. 'Everyone's done something he's ashamed of by the time he's fifteen. I'll bet this guy's no exception. Hell, we'll find something good on him and we'll barbecue his ass in molasses if he dares to open his great big mouth!'

They sat in the octagonal glass room, having what the Squadron

Leader insisted was a 'Council of War'. It was a week after the receipt of old Andrew Ross's letter, and ten o'clock on an early July evening after a day of rare heat. The visitors had all gone back to their hotels, chalets, tents and caravans. It was still bright daylight and the birds were still singing and it was one of those days near midsummer when there would be a shimmer of light on grass and road and hedge, almost the whole night. And by six o'clock the sun would be up again – and so it would be for all of this month in this magical northern turn of the year: the brief season in which the oldest of old men and women would feel at least a little of long-forgotten youth singing faintly in the blood. With perfect timing, Cal Jefferson had brought along a bottle of one of the rarest of old malt whiskies, the true usquebaugh water-of-life, and the four men sipped it very sparingly and carefully and felt their spirits lifted just a finger's breadth above the prosaic world as they talked and planned. This and the magic of the fading day made light work of the editing re-writing and re-editing of the careful letter in reply to Andrew Ross. The old Canadian was to be offered a week at Cal's hotel and a tour of his old home ground with David Henderson to assist him. In the enchantment of those moments Henderson felt an almost sacrilegious reluctance to broach the next subject of the meeting: the activities of the young Andrew Ross of forty-eight years ago but he forced himself into the impiety.

'I struck lucky almost at once,' he reported. 'I'll tell you something before I get into the story, though. I've always found it a particularly difficult concept – as I've no doubt you have, too – to visualise little old ladies, all prim in their go-to-church Sunday outfits, as the jolly sensual doxies many of them undoubtedly were, fifty or so years ago. I mean, there they are, cheeks like winter-stored apples, benign and grandmotherly or strict and shrivelled – but fifty or so years ago on enchanted summer nights like this one they were with their young men, hot and shy and daring everything in the fields and heather – '

'Is the poetry really necessary?' said Simon brutally. 'Can't we just, what I mean, get on with it, David?'

'Shame,' said Cal. 'Go on.'

'Yes. Well. I just want you to remember those nights in midsummer of fifty years ago because I have discovered – and it woke up a feeling of prudery and shock in me which I didn't know existed — that there's hardly been a marriage in this area within living memory in which the bride has not gone to the altar pregnant with a Praetorian Guard of parents standing tight-lipped by and some young man desperate, caught, his wenching days over before they've fairly begun.

'And so it was in Andrew Ross's day.'

Cal was the first there. 'Oh ho,' he said, with big coarse innuendo, 'searchay la dame, eh?'

'Er. Searchay, indeed, Cal. She is Effie MacGregor of this parish, mother of five, grandmother of a dozen, sits every Sunday in the third pew back from the front among lots of relatives at the Achnairn parish church, who was a winsome fifteen-year-old next door neighbour of Andrew Ross until these forty-eight years ago. They sat at adjacent desks in school and for a year, well, this being Kincardine and not Kentucky, he didn't carry her books home from school, Cal, but he carried a torch, by golly. Talking to Effie now you still get an inkling – nay, more than an inkling – of the raven-haired flirty temptress she must have been then. She's got a lovely sense of humour. And I swear there's still a look in that undimmed moss-green eye of hers that reminds you very forcefully of the witch she once was.

'It was certainly all too much for the young Andrew. I don't know the details – and I don't want to. But one thing's certain: on a night just like this, some forty-eight years ago, young Andrew and Effie did not come home from school for supper to either of their families after the end of term school hop – and did not, indeed, come home at all that night. They appeared at their respective homes in the small hours of the morning, and there was hell to pay in both families. Both young people kept their mouths shut, though, but five months later the evidence of what they had been up to that night was too obvious to be ignored any longer and there was a meeting of the families. Effie, of course, was under the age of consent which, even in Scotland at that time was sixteen – it was eighteen in England

– and so was young Andrew. What they had done was not only an offence against local morals. More seriously, it was actually against the law. Either of them – but almost certainly it would have been Andrew (because there isn't any equality of the sexes even yet in these cases) – was in danger of attracting the attention of the bloke Swacky refers to as the Procurator Physical and of being brought in front of a juvenile court and sent to an approved school. Of course this is the power that, even yet, makes escape damn near impossible for young village lotharios: most marriages around here are not made in Heaven but in the shadow of the Procurator. I don't know, of course, what was said between the two families but it would have been the usual intimidating stuff and presumably an agreement was reached – the usual one.

'But here's why the thing is remembered to this day by every contemporary of Effie and Andrew. Andrew's parents did an absolutely unheard-of thing for those days. They gave their agreement and promise of marriage between their son and Effie – and, a week before the due date they suddenly emigrated to Canada taking, of course, randy Andy with them. Effie was found a husband in a hurry but she's never forgotten Andrew and, judging by her interest in the idea that he might be coming over here, I would say she hasn't forgiven him, either.'

'She tell you all this?' Cal said in wonder.

'Oh, she's the most modern up-to-date old lady I've ever met, and the frankest. People, myself included, tend to forget that Highlanders were, until twenty years ago, about the most isolated people in Europe. Then everything arrived all at once, almost in a weekend: television, miniskirts and hotpants, public streetcorner couplings and caressings, the whole Permissive Society, women actually sitting down in pubs and drinking beer like the men, all when it was getting rather old hat everywhere else. They just took a great big horrified gulp and swallowed it whole, including a lot of stuff that wasn't really acceptable behaviour down South – but they weren't to know it. Like people everywhere who've been left behind and then have suddenly caught up with social trends, they're the most modern thing around. Effie told me the whole thing without a blush.

Her mother would have resisted red hot pincers in the flesh rather than confess a word of it.'

'I'm shocked, man,' Cal said.

'Did you really tell her her faithless Andrew was going to be back in town?' Simon said.

'I only hinted it was possible. I don't know what the statute of limitations is on breach of promise cases but it must have passed the limit ages ago. But I wouldn't think Effie gives a damn about the law. If Andrew shows his face around here and Effie hears of it, I really wouldn't like to be in his shoes.'

If moral blackmail didn't work, though, bribery might, thought Cal, and made his dispositions accordingly. Ten per cent of the first year's take on the Comet Trail would add up to between £10,000 and £20,000, Cal reckoned, and if that was a price to pay to avoid the collapse of the enterprise it would be cheap at the price. Most people in this world, thought Cal sourly, could be induced to remain silent on some moral matter for a year's salary – particularly if that sum was in cash and not credit: an untaxed gift rather than a taxable profit. Cash, good old greasy, fingered, used bucks were about the most difficult things to come by in this usurers' world and even a small amount of this rare commodity to spend as you like on whatever you liked with no percentage to pay to bank or building society or government, was the most powerful force on Earth. If that were not true Cal himself had learned nothing and understood nothing in his fifty-six years of wheeling and dealing and manipulating his fellow men. The only problem, though, was how to open the negotiations, how to approach Andrew and offer him the money. He was bound to accept it, if it was done right, but there would remain the age-old universal problem: once he had accepted the bribe, how did you ensure that he stuck to the terms of any promises he made? What sanctions could be invoked to make sure he kept them? Both the offering of the bribe and the accepting of it were actions right outside the orthodox workings of the law – not illegal, but certainly disreputable – and the conventions of the law would look on the users of such practices as social vagabonds. Cal could fairly easily take a clandestine record of the deal which could, perhaps, be used to embarrass Andrew if he tried to renege on it, but that was the extent of the sanction. Cal had a deeply-rooted objection, born of long years in business, to entering into a deal which was binding on one side only. 'Jefferson's Second Law of Business Practice,' he enunciated. 'If there's a possibility, somewhere, in any deal, for someone to be screwed, make sure you're the screwer, rather than the screwee.'

And so the three-pronged defence plan against Andrew Ross's disclosures – moral blackmail by Henderson, bribery by Cal – was completed by cajolery by Squadron Leader Hugh Ross. As a local man nearly contemporary with Andrew, indeed sharing the same surname (though that was no cause for remark in an area in which half the population of a village could share a surname) the Squadron Leader was judged the most likely to succeed in the 'good guy' role of gentle persuader. As Henderson put it to him: 'Just take him to one side and remind him what a poor place, financially, the Highland area is – not much work for bright youngsters, not much money for what work there is, little land worth cultivating, industries which arrive and then, as soon as their government grants run out, depart – and throw yourself and ourselves on his mercy. Not you, really. I think you ought to take the role of a benign and fatherly observer of our pranks. We've been rather naughty lads and pulled a bit of a scientific fraud on the gullible public but, hell, they're most of them only Sassenachs and Yanks, and it's in a good cause. After all, they got away with the fantasy of the Loch Ness Monster for half a century and that never did anyone any harm. People have to have something mysterious to marvel at so as to enliven their dull lives. All that sort of thing.'

The Squadron Leader was silent for quite a long time. When, eventually, he spoke, it was in a soft, musing voice, almost as if he were speaking to himself and he had forgotten the others were there. They had to lean forward to hear what he was saying. 'I think I remember the young Andrew,' he said. 'Half a century and a war ago. The world and the Highlands were different places then and us Highlanders knew precious little of what went on in the big world beyond our mountains. Except that from time to time they came up looking for boys to be soldiers and off we went, generation after generation, and precious few ever came home. Andrew's father, if I remember him, was a bit of a freethinker, ahead of his neighbours, and he wasn't the sort of fellow to obey the Call. I think that was one of the reasons they suddenly upped sticks and went to Canada. Andrew's and Effie's predicament must have been another reason. I suppose they thought they'd avoid the results of theirs and Andrew's mistakes and the mistakes of the politicians who were leading us back into war for the second time in a generation.'

The old man sighed gently and was silent for a while. 'Am I mistaken in supposing the summers were warmer then and the winters colder and shorter and drier? It seems, when I think back, that laughter was louder and longer and the tears dried more quickly. I remember, at this time of year, taking the short cut over the fields to the school over what is now a bog and Andrew must have been amongst us. Do I see him in my mind's eye: a bulky, round, red fair-haired loon who was always daffin' with the lassies? Once too often, it seems.' He squared his shoulders, straightening up, and his eyes focused abruptly on his listeners and he smiled a small shy smile.

'Aye,' he said. 'I'll talk to Andrew. I'll remind him of those old happy days in a land that's gone. I think he'll listen.'

Where, thought Henderson, have all those summer holiday landscapes with their painful joys and dreadful poignancies, gone? Did they exist at all outside the nostalgia of memory or are they something the mind, soured by disappointment and numbed by failures and the awful sense of time irretrievably passing, creates in order to make the journey bearable?

CHAPTER TWELVE

Andrew Ross arrived at the height of the short Highland summer. The iron song of the tractor was sounding on every little farm and croft as the hay grass was being cut at that frantic speed which indicates the distrust inherent in all farmers in the vicissitudes of the climate. The valleys and straths were full of the spicy odour of new-cut grass and the acrid smell of burnt diesel fuel – a benediction and a curse inextricably mingled in the modern manner.

Cal Jefferson's hotel limousine was at the Inverness Airport to meet the man from Canada and the driver of it had no difficulty in picking out the expatriate Highlander. The plane which brought him was full of oil company executives, the new husbandmen of the North Sea, engineers and sharp-eyed usurers from the City of London and even if Andrew had not been of retirement age and, in addition, wearing a tartan tam o'shanter of a sort that no resident Scot would put upon his head, he would still have stood out from his fellow passengers by virtue of the American cut of his holiday clothes, his relaxed style and the curiosity he showed in the scene and the people around him.

'Mighty nice of your boss to lay on a car for me,' he said when the driver picked him out. And, as he settled himself democratically in the front passenger seat – 'He a local fella?' He seemed intrigued to discover that Mr Jefferson was a fellow

North-American – 'From the wrong side of the border, though, eh?' he observed with a chuckle.

What Cal saw when he greeted Andrew on the steps of his barn hotel was a short, fit, merry-looking man with very shrewd grey eyes and no trace at all of the accents of his boyhood. He was very Canadian, very tough-seeming and quite open and ingenuous. This last quality of innocence and honesty worried Cal a good deal. 'I always find guys like this the most difficult to deal with,' he told Henderson a little later. 'No corners or angles to hang anything on, no cracks to put a wedge in. Guy like that makes no sense in the world of business that I know: nothing you can predict. No obvious greed. I distrust it intensely.' And so he switched with no perceptible meshing of gears into his bluff, boisterous apple-pie American mode, full of bonhomie and homely enthusiasms. Thus he, bear-like, placed one meaty arm around Andrew's shoulders and bore him along to his residents' bar on a tide of energy and talk.

'Hoo, boy,' he said, 'if you're fixing to pull the rug out from under our little tourist boom here you may as well have a good look, first, at what you're goin' to flush down the tubes. What'll you have, Andrew? Twenty good malts here. Bourbon if you prefer it.'

A slight slow smile turned up the corners of Andrew Ross's mouth. 'Just a glass of water, please. And maybe you'd better show me your caves, first, before we come to any big decisions, Mr Jefferson.'

('Water! Water, when there's all that good free malt!' Cal complained unbelievingly to Henderson later that night. 'This guy's not real. How can we deal with him?')

It was an evening of clear skies and calm after a morning of rain and Andrew made them stop many times on their way up to look down on the panorama of green fields just beginning to turn to summer ripeness, the surrounding forests and the dying gold of the broom and whin which spread wider as they mounted ever higher. And when they came to Cnocdruidh and soon to the Caves themselves with a straggling rump of the last of the day's visitors coming away from them, he stood looking at them for minute after minute without speaking.

'Well, Mr Ross. Well?' said Henderson at last.

The old Canadian seemed to come back from somewhere or somewhen far away, for he looked up at Henderson uncomprehendingly for a moment and, for a few seconds, his eyes did not see him. Then he was abruptly back in the present, on Cnocdruidh in the gloaming with the sentinel pines close-gathered around in solemn array.

'Oh, aye,' he said, and he spoke for the moment in the accents of his boyhood. 'It is the very same place.' And, wonderingly, 'It hasn't changed at all, not at all in all those years since Lachie Stewart and me rolled that boulder over the hole.'

Cal reported back to the Cabal twelve hours later. 'I can't make no impression on the guy whatsoever,' he said. 'I tried him with dough – hinted at it, rather than offered it, you know. Told him what we'd spent and how much we hoped to make. Sort of explained how it started off as, well, almost sort of a joke but how it grew into a game of what-if-we-could and from that into a why-not. The old bastard just looked at me, heard me out, nodded, ah-hahed like a good un and said he had more money than he knew what to do with, or words to that effect. And then he said, after one of those long pauses of his, in which he seems to go right away from you: 'I don't believe, Mr Jefferson, there is anything left on God's good earth which I could be offered which would induce me to change my mind about anything I believed to be wrong.' 'Trouble is,' added Cal, 'I like the guy despite his presbyterian morality and his saintly damn honesty. I keep getting the feeling that there must be a normal, rules-bending earthy guy inside. I'll tell you this, though: he's a helluva bright fella. I mean he was on to my ploy before I'd even put it to him and he'd rung up the No Sale sign before he even knew what was on offer. I reckon, Dave, it's over to you and you'll just have to get your ass into gear and make your pitch for all our sakes. I wish you luck.'

But David Henderson, as he reported later, never got the chance to make that pitch nor, after the first few minutes' talk alone with Andrew could he have dreamt of trying it. He and the old Canadian met by arrangement at Simon Briggs's hotel and had lunch together – a lunch which Andrew insisted on paying for. Henderson immediately taxed him about the Caves, for there was no point in pretending that they were not uppermost in everyone's minds. Was he absolutely sure they were those he and Lachie had played in as boys? Was there no chance of a mistake? Andrew had the chance, then, of letting everyone off the hook and he took so long before he replied that, for a while, Henderson thought he was going to give that chance. He sipped his glass of water, laid it down and studied it reflectively for many moments as if, in its tilting lucent depths, there was some chance of reading the future. Then he said: 'No, Mr Henderson, there's no chance of a mistake – unless you can find another cave on Cnocdruidh. I'm sorry.'

And when Henderson asked him if he had been down into the Caves yet he said: 'I don't think there'd be a lot of point in that, sir, do you? It wouldn't exactly convince me, would it? I think I'd rather remember them the way they were.'

Henderson told the others, later: 'I was wondering how the hell I could raise the subject of the Effie MacGregor scandal with him, and every time I thought of it my bowels shrivelled. It seemed an easy thing to do when he was a far-away threatening figure and the confrontation was weeks in the future. But he's far too decent a man, too wise and too truly . . . an old-fashioned word . . . dignified to do such a thing to. So there was I, squirming with the thought of having to report back to you lot that I'd been too cowardly even to try my great ploy and torn by the even worse possibility of trying to clobber this nice old mannie with an ancient scandal, and then, as if he could read my mind – and I truly think he did, because I never gave him the least hint of what I was trying to do – he reached across the table and put his hand on mine for a moment and looked me in the eye. And, apropos of nothing, he said, as far's I can remember it: "I'm going to see an old friend of mine this afternoon, so we'll have to cut lunch a wee bit short, Mr Henderson. Perhaps you know her – Effie MacGregor?" And while I was figuratively picking myself up off the floor and trying to get my lower jaw back into contact with my upper, he went on in that gentle musing tone of his, as if he's looking on from a great distance at his own and our antics: "We haven't met in fifty years and we parted in the midst of a bit of a scandal which wouldn't, I'm sure, interest you, Mr Henderson. But it was quite a cause célèbre at the time – the usual rustic story of a devil-may-care lad and a careless lassie in a summer just like this one, long, long ago. She forgave me a long time ago, of course; we've been faithful correspondents for many years but in all this time I've never seen her. I must admit I'm a wee bit excited about our reunion at long last. Can you understand that, Mr Henderson?"

'Well, that was my bum most definitely out of the window and I just made sort of inarticulate noises for the rest of the lunchtime until it was time for him to go. What I would like to know is, even if he guessed we were going to hit him with the Effie MacGregor scandal, how the hell did he know I was the one who was going to do it? I tell you, it's eerie. I think old Andrew's a wizard: he's got what the Gaels call the *taischiteraugh*, shadow-sight, or what's known as second-sight. He's probably the seventh son of a seventh son and communicates routinely with the wee folk who live under the ground . . .'

The next time they all saw Andrew was at the Squadron Leader's home, in his spacious sitting room and although it was meant to be an informal occasion, there was a slight air of formality about it. By a common impulse everyone remained standing; it was clear it was to be a brief gathering and the Squadron Leader and Andrew, who stood at the heart of the room with their backs to the huge mantelpiece, wasted no time on trivialities. Andrew, with no preliminaries, very gently and with a total lack of self-consciousness, told them very simply why their ploys had not worked. First, he said with a glance at Cal, he was very rich indeed and had no need nor, indeed, any wish for any more money or possessions. What he would like, but no man could give him, was more time and more wisdom to spend that which he had. Secondly, glancing towards Henderson who fidgeted and looked at his feet, no confrontation nor any scandal connected with his wild youth could touch him now. He had, in fact, paid a call on 'an old and very dear friend of his youth' and they had cried and hugged and laughed over those long-ago indiscretions. 'And if only it was suitable or possible we would repeat them tomorrow and rejoice,' he said. And then Andrew grew a little solemn and slow. Thirdly, he said – and he went over to the Squadron Leader and the two old men clasped hands and looked into each other's eyes – thirdly, there was no need at all to appeal to his sensibilities as an ex-Highland man and a Good Guy.

'Of course you're never going to get away with it. Someone will blow the whistle on you: someone amongst you, or someone from without. The scheme is too big, too many people already know about it. There are too many loopholes. If I have learned one thing in all my years of dealing with people great and small, wise and foolish, it is that they cannot keep a secret. A secret is a boring thing in itself – a seed, a shoot without a flower. It is the sharing of it which confers on a man or a woman such a delicious sense of conspiracy and power. Like money, it has to be spent to be enjoyed; it is a currency without value unless it is in circulation.

'But it will not be me who puts it into circulation. I will not tell your secret. I wish you all the luck in the world and I thank you, I thank you from the bottom of my heart for giving me one of the happiest weeks of my life on my first, last and only visit to my old home. Hugh, here, will explain the rest. Myself, I . . . I have . . . no time.'

Then he raised his glass and made them all drink to the success of the Cnocdruidh Caves and soon afterwards he left, driving rapidly away in Cal's hotel limousine with Cal's driver at the wheel and never once looking back.

When they turned back to Hugh his eyes were moist but he was smiling. 'He was, indeed, the lad I remember running beside me through the fields on the way to school,' he said, 'but there was never the slightest chance – nor the slightest need – of us suborning him. He told me to tell you he's sorry for stringing you along a bit but he was enjoying himself too much to give up the game right away. As he said, there's only one thing he wants and that, he can't get – not money, not love, not power: none of these things. What he wants is Time. And his time is up. He has, at the most, three or four months to live. He wanted to see his old home and to recapture some of the time that has gone before he dies.'

But David Henderson was thinking as they dispersed: which one among us was Andrew, with the wisdom which had settled on him as his time ran out, warning us about? Who would break the secret?

CHAPTER THIRTEEN

Letter from Alison Fraser to David Henderson, August 3rd.

Dear David,

Why haven't they found our Time Bomb yet? Did you bury it too deep? The kerfuffle in the academic world is settling down much too quickly, the way it always has a tendency to do, and, I suspect, in the mind of the public as well. Why aren't they digging? Somehow we must get old Mould up there again, soon. And what is the creature, Ryle, doing – selling tickets or getting boozed every night on good Scotch whisky? Next year, or the year after, won't do. See what you can do, short of digging up the bloody thing yourselves, to get things moving again.

Need I say that I'm longing to see you and, several times have been on the verge of making a clandestine visit – although I know perfectly well that in our part of the world it's impossible to blow your own nose without someone noticing it?

I don't think you're safe on your own. I think you need a good woman to look after you.

Love, Ally.

Swacky was delighted to be entrusted with another task. 'No problem at all,' he assured Henderson. 'First dark night, about two o'clock, over the wire and down the hole. That bugger, MacGillivray'll be night watchman and he couldn't spot a cow in a barn after dark. D'you want me to do anything else while I'm down there – stick a few more paintings on the walls, like?'

'Christ, no, Swacky. Just stir things up a bit, OK?'

A story in the Daily Telegraph newspaper, August 7th.

Vandals have broken into the caves at Cnocdruidh Hill in the north-east Highlands where the eminent archaeologist Dr Nathaniel Mould made a major discovery this year. A gate in the perimeter fence at the site was forced during the night and attempts appear to have been made to look for buried treasure.

It will be recalled that, not far from the site, on the Black Isle in Easter Ross-shire a Viking hoard of silver was discovered some twenty years ago by a ploughman which was worth more than £50,000 to the finder. And although the Cnocdruidh Hill discoveries are of a much earlier, neolithic, era it is thought that uninformed treasure hunters could have been hoping for a similar find.

Nothing seems to have been removed from the caves but part of the earth floor in the inner cave was dug up and rocks and earth have been thrown about in a clumsy attempt to find anything of value. Dr Mould, when contacted yesterday, said he was going up to the site immediately to assess the position.

'I am greatly worried,' he said. 'This is quite possibly the most important archaeological site in Britain currently being investigated and any disturbance caused by amateur treasure-seekers could do irreparable damage.' He blamed what he called: 'ridiculously over-enthusiastic publicity seeking on the part of the local community,' for creating a climate in which the vandalism could occur.

The discoveries at Cnocdruidh have set the British archaeological milieu in a ferment because the cave paintings and artifacts found there appear to pre-date other settled neolithic sites by some two thousand years and include the celebrated 'twin-circles' motif found on standing stones throughout the far north and, until now, thought to be of Pictish origin. But the same motif on the cave walls must have been placed there by a much earlier hand.

Much academic argument, too, has been sparked off by the huge winged and helmeted figure of a man found in the inner cave, which some scholars at first tentatively interpreted as the Graeco-Roman god Hermes, but is now thought to predate the Greek heroic period by many hundreds, if not more than a thousand years.

A growing stream of interested amateurs has been visiting the site since early this year and several cults are showing signs of growing up around these discoveries. These include one group which believes the circles and helmeted figure are evidence of a visit in the prehistoric era by representatives of an alien civilisation either from our solar system or beyond it. Another group believes the circles are evidence of a twin-headed comet which either struck, or passed close by, the Earth, causing such disasters as the Biblical Flood. These theorizings are totally dismissed by orthodox academics and by persons of Dr Mould's academic standing as too absurd to comment on at all.

This paper-thin gold plate, ten inches by eight and weighing about six ounces, represented an investment by Cal Jefferson and David Henderson of about two thousand pounds and was all that remained of a gold 'hunter' watch case that had belonged to Henderson's grandfather and a snuff box with a hole in it which Cal claimed had been caused by a rifle bullet during the American Civil War. The re-smelting and purifying of the gold and the hot-rolling of it into its strange geometrical shape had, in view of the rather crude alchemy which was possible in Henderson's kitchen and the difficulty they had had in obtaining books on metallurgy, taken several weeks. And, always a perfectionist in matters of detail, Cal had insisted on the thing being done and re-done at least a dozen times until he was satisfied that it was done as well as they could.

'It behooves us,' he had said, slipping into his role of backwoods American hick, as the painstaking process drew itself out, 'not to let down the generosity of your grand-pappy nor to have caused my great-uncle Herbert to have yielded up his life in vain on the killing fields of Saratoga. Besides, these scientific smart-asses will be testing it every which way.'

The gold of Cal's snuff box contained a large fraction of silver and that of Henderson's 'hunter' a fraction of copper which, they learned from their researches, was always admixed with the pure gold in historical times to give it strength. A trace of either of these would rouse the suspicions immediately and fatally of the informed investigator. Each object had to be heated to within a degree or two of the melting point of gold but below that of silver or copper then briefly raised just above the melting point of gold and the pure gold poured off. There was a faintly occult air to this alchemy as all this was done late at night in a much-prized cast iron ashtray in the shape of a three-legged pot of the sort supposed to have been used in adventure stories by cannibals to boil missionaries in, and which Henderson kept as a memento of his days in Africa.

They had read in some work on ancient metallurgy that gold was beaten into thin plate by placing it in a sandwich of ox hide leather and then hammering it until it spread out into a sheet a hundred times thinner than paper. It proved extraordinarily difficult to obtain locally leather of the appropriate thickness and elasticity but eventually Cal's treasured cowboy jacket was enlisted into service, dissected and cut into appropriately sized bits. The pure, very hot, gold which had been laboriously flattened and spread by the use of Henderson's glass rolling pin on the top of an old marble wash-stand, producing many scalds and scolds in the process ('All the important technical things in this plot seem to involve the use of my kitchen machinery,' Henderson observed) was then laid between these emblems of the wild west and hammered for hour after hour. The result was far better than either of them had imagined. By some magical properties of the leather padding which the ancients had known so well but which modern technological man found hard to account for, the gold at the end of all this lay thin and flat and even, ready for whatever was to be inscribed thereon.

And now, having lain beneath the earth for nearly a year, like a slowly ticking bomb, its time was come and it needed only Dr Mould's prying fingers to release its energies.

Dr Mould's second assault on the Cnocdruidh Caves took place in a fine glare of publicity. The news media, already intrigued by the cult growing up around the winged figure and the twin 'saucers', had the extra peg of the treasure hunters' break-in on which to hang their stories. A small television crew had joined the photographers, professional and freelance, the local newspaper reporters, stringers and radio reporters in a busy little media circus to record his hasty return to the site. Interest was clearly growing. Martin Ryle, red and flustered amid all this ferment, hopped around his master who was embarrassed, annoyed, but showing some evidence of ambivalence, by all this attention. As ever, he was finding it difficult to reconcile the need which his calling had for publicity with the form that attention took. It could not be managed or predicted, could only be gently persuaded. This mixture of attitudes manifested itself in a brusqueness which only just fell short of rudeness. Trapped for a moment in front of the cameras, microphones and notebooks he said crossly: 'I don't know what you all expect to see. An archaeological dig is a slow and meticulous process. We don't just take a pick and shovel and throw clods of earth around, you know. We may find nothing more at all – ever. Or, if we do, it'll probably take weeks and be something so small and uninteresting – to you, that is, not to me – as a single tooth.'

'Or you might find the Ancient Astronaut's space helmet,' suggested one reporter in an attempt at waggishness – and the cameras were rewarded with a glare, eyebrows gathered, nostrils flared, which was the only photogenic thing they got that day.

Dr Mould was underestimating, however, his own serendipity – and the artfulness with which Swacky had vandalised the cave floor, leading him subliminally to the Time Bomb. It was not weeks or days but only a matter of hours before trowel and sieve and fine-bristled brush uncovered the outlines of the dull metal plaque which, upon being removed from the gritty earth with infinite delicate care, brought the reporters and picture-takers scooting back from Inverness to which, disappointed, they had repaired to try the limited pleasures offered by that miniature Presbyterian city. By the time they saw it the plate had been carefully cleaned (the dirt from it stored and labelled as if itself it were gold dust) but not otherwise scoured and the stained metal did not have the exciting gleam of gold which the newsmen might have expected. But its deeply inscribed whorls, strokes and patterns were clearly visible.

Almost the oddest thing about it was its shape. It was not a common earthly shape. Its angles were all wrong. It had five sides, one curved and four straight, none of the same length and disturbingly asymmetrical. The human brain seeks, indeed *needs* symmetry and balance and searches for it even in natural panorama, picking unconsciously those views for favourites which show a 'natural balance' of hill, forest, water, valley. To create the antithesis of this balance, as Henderson and Cal discovered, is very hard to do; the hand and eye keep trying to snap back to a plan, hating anarchy.

Dr Mould's news conference took the form of a little lecture, incomprehensible to all save one or two of the newsmen. He spoke as clearly as he could and with manifest effort, in words of one syllable each as if to a group of badly educated children. And while this was undoubtedly the level of comprehension of most of his audience, even they realised they were being talked down to and resented it mightily.

'The plaque,' he said, 'is of gold. It does not look like gold because it is stained with dirt from the cave floor. The earliest gold found in Britain until now consists of some items of jewellery dated at 2,700 B.C. or thereabouts. If this is of the same date as the paintings and other artifacts – er, objects – found at this site it will be at least a thousand years older than that. In effect it pushes back the date of the neolithic – er, New Stone Age – by that same period of a thousand years. It would certainly be the oldest gold object found in Europe, perhaps in the whole world.

'The plaque itself is of an unusual shape which, at first sight, gives the impression that some part of it is missing. Perhaps it is. But in the necessarily brief examination we have been able to give it, it seems quite likely that it is complete and that its unusual shape was intended. This shape resembles nothing that I have seen or read about from this or any other era. There are marks and shapes engraved on the surface of the plaque, including a double circle and zigzag inscription similar to that on the cave wall. There are other marks which seem to be intentional, rather than a result of scratching, weathering and abrasion – but that is all I can say without further examination.'

And try they never so hard, the newsmen could not get another word out of him.

Television news that evening had a brief account of the finding of the plaque with a glimpse of it, artfully sidelighted to show the linked-circles symbols. The other marks and symbols, the whorls and spidery lines which were reminiscent of runic inscriptions, did not reproduce on the television screen. There were a few seconds of interview with Dr Mould in which he merely repeated his speculation that the plaque, if contemporaneous with the cave paintings, was the oldest metal object discovered.

'Oldest in Britain?' asked the interviewer.

'The oldest anywhere,' the archaeologist replied, and again refused to be coaxed into saying anything further.

(Watching this item, Henderson, Simon and Cal jumped up and did a little Highland Schottische around Cal's desk. 'If that don't get publicity everywhere where people can read, nothing will,' Cal crowed.)

The neatest headline, in one of the more popular comics, was: 'MOULD STRIKES GOLD.' The most far-fetched was a journal with pretensions towards intellectuality which sought to compare the plaque with such other survivals from past civilisations as the Phaestos Disk of Minoan Crete and the Rosetta Stone.

But one of the shrillest tabloids the next day scored notably over the rest by leading not with an account of the finding of the plaque itself but with the reaction to it of an individual called Daniel Beardsley, the slightly wild-eyed paramount chief of a tribe of Ancient Astronauts who called themselves, quite seriously, the Sons of the Comet and who had settled in the vicinity in a motley collection of campers, vans, tents, caravans and 'mobile homes'. Daniel was very tall, very thin and with hair and skin so unpigmented that, were it not for a pair of startling viridescent eyes, he seemed at first sight to be an albino. He had come stalking up the hill to see David Henderson at the beginning of June, hard on the heels of the first reporters, and had uninhibitedly introduced himself as a follower of arcane mystical cults, 'looking for an answer to some of the mysteries of this world,' as he said, adding disarmingly, 'you'll probably think I'm a nut case, but I assure you I'm quite harmless, just a confused and diligent searcher after truth.' Henderson liked him on sight and went to some trouble to find him somewhere to pitch his camp and to advise him where to go for his supplies. For Daniel, with all his wholehearted enthusiasms, was a man of no small education and could produce an impressive array of fact, extrapolation from fact and inferences from them which could be quite persuasive even when he was pressing his theories to the limit. He was not, as many an amiable English eccentric, given over to the extremes of wild surmise. He did not go along with the Flying Saucers have Landed and Taken Me On a Trip to Venus school of fantasy. He did not believe in mysterious forces under the Caribbean which sucked ships and aeroplanes down into a vortex, preferring the more prosaic explanation that it was an area of unpredictable weather. He was a romantic – but he liked a bit of evidence.

He excelled himself in the interview. There was a picture of him standing with the background of Cnocdruidh behind him, his long grey locks floating around his head, looking like some Biblical prophet as depicted by Victorian illustrators of the Bible. 'We believe,' he was reported as saying, 'that this gold plaque is the last link in the chain of evidence which points conclusively to the fact that the Cnocdruidh Cave is a record of the most important event in human history and the mainspring of all our religions and myths of Gods descending to the earth. It is a record of the coming to earth six thousand years ago of men from beyond our planet. The winged and helmeted figure of

"Hermes" is clearly an attempt by the savage inhabitants of this land at that time to depict one of these travellers. The twin circles and the "lightning" depict their vehicle and the attempt to describe its propulsion system. How would such people, I invite you to ask yourselves, have tried to draw a modern astronaut returning to earth as they do today in an Apollo Shuttle?

'But this gold plaque is the clearest evidence of all. People of the earth at the time this was made had no knowledge of smelting metal and no means of obtaining gold-bearing ore even if they had had that knowledge. We believe this plaque and the symbols on it are a message from the stars. What that message is, we may or may not ever know, for, even yet, we have not been able to translate the script from the temple of Knossos on Crete which was most definitely written by men, and only 1,600 years before Christ.'

Daniel continued with some quite well-documented theorising on current archaeological fashion, speculating that the builders of the underground houses, the chambered cairns, the stone-circles and cromlechs, had moved in neolithic times from the north of Britain and Europe to southern Europe, not as had been popularly supposed, the other direction, carrying the germ of civilisation with them to the Mediterranean and across it, where it flourished mightily in the sands of Mesopotamia and Egypt.

'The great neolithic builders, settlement, farming, the working of metal – all of human culture began here when the minds of men which had lain unawakened for millennia were awakened by these visitors from space,' Daniel concluded.

As Henderson said on the telephone to Alison that evening: 'He couldn't have done better if we'd programmed him ourselves, wound him up and set him walking. It's worked out so well that I've got a creepy feeling about it.'

'I know what you mean,' Alison said. 'You get a horrible feeling that something's bound to go wrong.'

Meanwhile, at tea-room, Bar, Caravan site, hotels and Comet Trail, the tempo of business, already brisk, was building up pressure by the day. Little cottages which had never opened their doors to strangers found bed-and-breakfast space for those who arrived hourly to visit the Caves. Cal Jefferson, who had been trying for some weeks to persuade his friend to look after his operation while he spent the obligatory six months-and-a-day stipulated by the United States Inland Revenue Service back in his homeland, gave Henderson the benefit of an analysis he had been making on the motives of his customers. 'When people used to come here for the Loch Ness Monster promotion, ninety per cent of them didn't really believe there was any monster under the loch,' he said. 'But they came, knowing it was all probably a hype because in our heart of hearts we all of us want to believe in something mysterious and exciting. It makes life more interesting. And they don't really believe in old Daniel, up there' – and he nodded his head towards the north-east where Daniel Beardsley's camp was growing larger by the day – 'and his Ancient Astronauts. But so long as no-one can disprove it, why, it makes life just that little bit more full of wonder.

'For me, too,' he added, and in the pause which followed, the myriad jingle of coins into tills and the clink of glasses and of knives and forks on plates, confirmed his words.

FALL

CHAPTER FOURTEEN

'The heart is deceitful above all things and desperately wicked. Who can know it? I, the Lord, search the heart, I try the reins, even to give every man according to his ways and according to the fruit of his doings.

'As the partridge sitteth upon eggs and hatcheth them not; so he that getteth riches, and not by right, shall leave them in the midst of his days and at his end shall be a fool.'

These words of that mournful old prophet, Jeremiah, intoned from the pulpit of the Laidmore village church, seemed to Simon Briggs to be directed to him alone and to have been written especially for him. The Sunday sermon of the Reverend Marcus Mackenzie caught him in a mood in which he was at his most vulnerable, when he was already profoundly troubled by the deceit he and his peers had practised upon the archaeological establishment and the public. The profound disequilibrium at Simon's core, that volatility which threw him from hope to despair, to guilt and despondency, had him, this day, in its toils. And now that his crushing financial burdens were over and riches were pouring in from his crammed bars and his overflowing rooms, he was casting about for an excuse to feel guilty. The Reverend Mackenzie's sermon, delivered in that special minatory voice in which preachers talk to God, resounded in his soul and worked the change in him. For, though he was not a religious man in the orthodox sense of regular worship and ritual, he had always carried within him a worrying consciousness of incompleteness and a need for an exposition of mysteries which science and logic could not explain.

The preacher's voice, now lecturing God on exactly what his prophet had meant by his ambiguous and equivocal words, faded into a sort of twittering background to Simon's thoughts as he applied Jeremiah's words to his life. In the hissing silence of his thoughts he suddenly had a vision of Hell as an actual place of torment awaiting the souls and bodies of those who had sinned. A picture arose from his childhood of himself on Judgement Day, summoned in an instant, out of sleep, standing before the ranks of angels and that dazzling throne, alone in his pyjamas while God itemized from a vast ledger the sins and peccadilloes he had committed: an old atavistic dread which caught him in its seductive grip, urging self-abnegation and repentance.

Simon knew he had sinned and the chief of these sins, because it had brought him rich rewards, was the deceit he had aided, abetted and profited by in the seeding of the Cnocdruidh Caves. 'He that getteth riches, and not by right, shall leave them in the midst of his days . . . ' It could not be mere coincidence that words so apposite were produced by a preacher who could have no inkling of the deception and no knowledge of Simon's part in it.

As the rest of that Sunday went by in the routine tasks involved in running his hotel Simon became increasingly obsessed by the message he thought he had discerned in the prophet's words. By the time he had tucked his clients in for the night and supervised the closing of his bars and the cleansing of his kitchen, he could think of very little else. He believed that his soul was in danger and that he must make expiation for his wrong-doing. He spent a sleepless night dominated with confused and fantastic visions of Hell, of redemption, of reward and punishment chasing themselves through his brain and when he arose in the morning some chemistry of the mind had wrought a great change within him. As soon as his duties permitted he left the hotel and went to see David Henderson who, the moment he saw him, pale and filled with an inner excitement which Henderson fancied he could feel throbbing within him at the touch of his hand, knew that something was seriously amiss with his friend.

'I have to speak to you right away, in private,' Simon said. 'What I mean – I've decided what we are doing is wrong and must be put right. We are in great danger – '

'Danger? Danger of what, Simon?'

'Of Hellfire. Of Damnation. I've thought it all out.'

And then Henderson knew it was trouble, and trouble of the very worst kind: not rational, logical, predictable trouble which could be met and analysed and dealt with, but trouble springing from that ancient seat of instincts which knows no rules and is the strongest and the most irrational force in human life. He had planned for every other threat, of betrayal, of carelessness, of accident. It had never crossed his mind that the most serious attack would come from this quarter where neither sense nor self-interest could prevail.

'Oh, Simon, Simon,' he said, 'who have you been talking to? What've you been reading? Hellfire? Damnation? For God's sake, you're sounding for all the world like one of those old-time street corner revivalists. You know – Repent, for the Kingdom of Heaven is at hand!'

Simon interrupted in a kind of fierce whisper. 'I knew this would be your attitude, David. But this is not the time for jokes. I tell you I'm serious – more serious than I've ever been in my life and you'll not talk me out of it.'

Henderson drew him into his little study, a room of books and papers, two comfortable chairs and a desk, and made him coffee while Simon talked on and on. 'I've always, what I mean, nearly believed in God and Creation and Heaven and Hell and an after-life. Sometimes I've believed it when, you know, there seems to be no other explanation for things. Other times, when the whole world seems in a mess, I've doubted it – doubted that there could possibly be a god supervising such a . . . muddle. But there've been other times, too, when there's wars and killing and things, I think I've understood the battle that's always going on between the forces of Good and Evil. And I've realised that it is all part of the workings of God. But yesterday I heard these words in Church . . . ' And to Henderson's pity and embarrassment he produced a Bible and found the passage in Jeremiah which had so moved him and read it out. 'When I heard these words I knew without any doubt why they were put into the mouth of Reverend Mackenzie. They were there for you and me and the others to hear. There's no doubt in my mind at all.'

David Henderson started to laugh, because he couldn't help himself, but one look at Simon's furious face shut him up immediately. 'I'm sorry, Simon,' he said, 'but no-one's read the Bible to me since I was a child. And if anyone was ever going to I would never have plumped for Jerry-bloody-miah. Oh, sorry, sorry. I really don't mean to give offence. But, look, Simon, there may be something – though I couldn't believe it myself – but there may be some mystery behind all this talk of prophets and rituals and sacrifice and sin. You know what my personal view is: I think it's nothing more than a human development of an instinct as old as, say, a bower bird's decoration of his nest. But surely it couldn't be so simple as you're making it – Satan and God at war over our allegiances . . . '

No, no, said Simon. The very imperfection of our ideas about God and the fact that we know we have those imperfections, were themselves evidence of the workings of God.

Henderson decided to abandon this casuistry and tried another tack. 'Well, then, Simon, let's suppose it is a conviction you have for the moment and that by tomorrow, or next week, you feel differently. It would be awful to throw everything away that we've worked for, just when it's bearing fruit, wouldn't it, when you might decide next week it was all a mistake? Think about it. Let it rest for a while. Come and talk about it again but, for the moment, let it lie. Let it grow or let it fade, but leave taking any action for a while.'

But Simon could not let it rest. He was not a brooding creature, he said. And it was clear that he was in the grip of a terrible zeal, a fierce need to act, to expiate which, like a long-smouldering fire, had suddenly burst into flame. Henderson found him obdurate.

'I must make confession,' he said.

Henderson stared at him. 'You haven't become a Roman Catholic, Simon? Forgive me, but the Presbyterian Church of Scotland doesn't hear confessions. That's popery – '

'I don't mean that sort of confession. I mean confession to the world at large – to the public, to the newspapers, to the television.'

'Confess what, though, Simon? Your sins? Which particular sins? Lust? Short-changing – though I'm sure you don't? Deceiving the Inland Revenue inspectorate, the VAT man?'

'Don't mock, David. I tell you I'm serious. I have to confess your, my, deception about all this – ' he waved a hand in the general direction of the Cnocdruidh Caves – 'this . . . swindle. I've sat up most of the night trying to work out how much I've made out of it – it's no easy matter calculating what the normal takings would have been and subtracting this from the increased business – and how I'm to give it all back. And who do I give it back to? You can do what you like with yours but I have to return it and tell the news media why I'm doing it.'

'Good God, Simon, you can't! D'you really think Jehovah gives a tuppenny damn about your cash-flow – ?'

'Everyone knows you've always been anti-religious,' Simon said.

'I don't know where you get that idea from, Simon. I'm greatly in favour of religion of almost all kinds, even if I don't have need of it myself. It's tremendously useful. It keeps thousands of people out of lunatic asylums – ' And was immediately sorry he'd said it.

'There you go,' shouted Simon, 'exactly what I said, mocking and scorning religious people. Blasphemy against God. I'm going.'

And he got up to go, but Henderson was angry, too, now and he detained him a little longer, standing between him and the door, and he, too, raised his voice, although he realised it was wrong and useless. 'Look here, Simon,' he said, 'you'll have to give up this stupid idea. I'm not going to let you throw everything away that we've worked for on such a silly whim. We're not going to let you. Do you hear me?' Because Simon did not seem to be listening. 'Do you hear, Simon? You can believe what you want. You can go and pray all day in Church or give all your wealth to the poor and go to be a missionary in bloody Matabeleland, but you'll have to leave us out of it, Simon.'

'But that is precisely what I cannot do,' said Simon, with the sort of mad certainty about everything which had descended on him. He spoke now in tones which had become calm and measured, almost placatory. 'I'm sorry the rest of you will be involved and I don't want to harm you but I must make my peace with my own soul. I advise you and the others to do the same.'

And no amount of exhortation, of reasoning, of sympathy and finally of rage could sway him in the least particular.

Hugh Ross said: 'Had a fella in my squadron during the war, went like that. Came back from a bombing mission over Hamburg in a badly damaged machine that ended up as a ball of flame at the end of the runway and he was the only one that survived. Not a scratch on him. He took it for a sign from the Almighty and refused to fly ever again. Ended up in the Loony Bin. No-one could talk him out of it.'

Hugh, it appeared to Henderson, was taking it very calmly. 'Are you suggesting we should try to get Simon committed?' he said.

'Oh, no chance of that, I should think. Religious mania's more or less sanctioned by the State, isn't it? Have to get half the population of the Highlands committed if that was the case. No, I was just trying to show you that when these chaps get this kind of a bug they've usually got it forever. They never seem to revert to normal again once they've heard the Voices or seen the Light. No, there's nothing to be done except stand up and take it. Pity though,' he said, looking around at his tastefully set-out dining room and thinking of his brand new kitchens which had been providing gourmet meals for the very rich. 'Pity – but we'll probably keep some of the trade. And all this is paid for. We'll look a bit foolish, though, David. We haven't done anything criminal, though, so far as I can see. We'd better treat it as a big joke and hope for the best.'

'You don't sound too surprised.'

'Well, I'm not, really, my boy. Remember what old Andrew Ross said in this very room – that we'd never get away with it? He warned us, if you remember, that one of us would break the secret. I had a pretty good idea, then, who it would be and I'm not too surprised. I've been rather waiting for it. But, by Jove, it's all been terrific fun. I'm glad we did it; it's really woken me up and given me a taste for life again and put off the day when I sink into old fogeyhood. In fact I don't believe I ever will, now. I've got a dozen things I want to do and probably won't have time for. But you'd better get around and tell the others so they can get plans made for how they're going to deal with it.

'A word, though. Don't be too sure of the outcome. The public's queer cattle, you know, and awful hard to predict.'

Swacky did not find it easy to understand. Religiosity was a familiar part of his life and he was used to the intense and cruel puritanism of the more primitive offshoots of the presbyterian sect. Himself, he had no reverence for ministers and priests, lumping them all together as killjoys and creatures of landlords, the police, Procurator Physicals and other instruments of institutionalised oppression. But the concept of a mature and sophisticated man such as Simon Briggs undergoing a radical religious conversion was something he found hard to grasp.

'This conversation of his,' Swacky said after a while. 'You can't talk him out of it, man?'

'Er, no, Swacky. He seems pretty well determined.'

'And will all these newspaper journalists and tee vee men believe what he says?'

'It seems extremely likely, Swacky. After all, he was in on the thing from the very beginning and knows all the nitty gritty details. He'll tell a pretty convincing story.'

They were sitting in the lounge bar of one of the smaller hotels – not Simon's – well away from the crowd of usual Friday night drinkers, talking in low conspiratorial voices. As they were talking one of Cal's Comet Trail buses went by the window, crammed to the doors with the curious and credulous, off on the first leg of a three-day tour of stone circles, weems and cromlechs and sculptured stones. When they returned, thought Henderson, would they be yelling for their money back and claiming they'd been swindled? Swacky, watching him and sipping his pint of beer, caught the thought.

'Aye,' he said, 'the wee bastard's going to throw the cat in the fire, right enough, if we let him.'

And these two, different in many ways, who between them had evolved the whole ploy, one the man of reflex action, the other a schemer and plotter, who had fathered it and nurtured it as their mutual trust and interdependence had grown along with it, let that thought hang in the air for a long beat.

Eventually –

'You could tell everyone he's gone mad,' said Swacky. 'That the drink and losing his wife was too much for his brain.'

In the public bar on the other side of the wall, where Swacky would much rather have been, the sounds of Friday night would be getting louder and taking on that peculiar cadence which is generated in Highland bars: a cacophony of sound punctuated by silences as anecdotes gleaned from the week's activities in township and field are heard in attentive silence followed by outbursts of laughter, sometimes mocking, sometimes appreciative, like some rolling turbulent sea. In one of these pauses Swacky said with utter seriousness: 'We could just kill the bastard. I know plenty places we could put the body.'

And while David Henderson stared at him, slack-jawed – 'Och, he's no bloody use to anyone and he's a misery to himself. People have been killed for a hoor-of-a-lot less than you and Cal and Rossie have spent on this thing. And if he's that keen on going to Heaven why the hell shouldn't we make his wish come true? Man, Davie, we'd be doing him, and ourselves, a favour!'

Cal Jefferson, when he was told, sat stock still in the big chair behind his desk for so long that Henderson thought for a moment that he might be going to have a fit. And then he thumped two mighty fists down on the table, threw back his head and roared with laughter. When he got his breath back he said, gaspingly: 'Oh boy.' And then, again: 'Oh boy.'

This was not at all the reaction Henderson had expected. Rage, despondency, yes. Amusement, no.

'What the hell are you laughing at, Cal?' Henderson said. 'I thought you'd be screaming the bloody place down.'

'Don't really know, Dave. I suppose it just struck me as exactly like the denouement of an old-style Hollywood movie – the Bad Guys caught out at the end and deprived of the dollars. Then I had a sudden mental picture, quite clear, of that stuffed shirt, Nathaniel Mould, looking like the biggest asshole since Piltdown Man.'

'But the money, Cal, the business!'

'Short of murdering the bastard, or hi-jacking him and keeping him locked away, I don't see there's anything we can do to stop him, once he's really made up his mind. And I'll tell you a thing, boy, speaking as a man who's made a few fortunes and lost a few: when you're dealing with the public you can't be sure of nothing. I'm not about to make noises as if I'm going down the tubes until I actually find myself sliding back downwards with nothing to hold on to. If I'm going to be dragged over the cliff it won't be without one helluva struggle. You'll see heel-marks all the way to the edge.'

CHAPTER FIFTEEN

Dear Ally,

Our balloon, if not already burst by the time you get this, is about to be. Simon Briggs has been Born Again (and not before time, I hear you cry) and has fallen victim to a bout of Godfearing honesty and a touch of the John-Three-Sixteens. If you don't know what that is, you heathen, look it up in your New Testament. If you have one.

Anyway, he says he's going to make a clean breast of the whole Cnocdruidh Caves deception to the news media and thus save his soul from Hell while conveniently laying up treasure in Heaven at the same time. I'm trying to write light-heartedly but really I'm pretty shattered. Everyone's spoken to Simon, but he's quite obdurate. The only one of us with a practical answer is Swacky, of course. He's made some pretty detailed plans for Simon to render his last and greatest service to mankind by submerging himself in a peat bog – with assistance. So far I've managed to restrain him but if you read a paragraph in the paper about Mysterious Disappearance of Northern Hotelier, burn this. It might be evidence.

All love, David.

At ten o'clock there was a persistent rapping on David Henderson's front door. When he opened it there was a familiar figure that swayed slightly as it stood in the porch framed in the crepuscular light. The end of the day glowed on the horizon beyond the hills to the west, brightly enough to make mere pinpricks of the stars and it would not be dark for long before the glow began slowly to brighten again in a few hours' time and the sun rose once more over field and loch and strath.

Swacky said, as he came in: 'I've got it all worked out, boss. Let's just sit down and have a dram of this, and I'll tell you how we're going to do it.' 'This' was a three-quarter-full bottle of whisky and, in his other hand, was a plastic bag which, from the noise it made as it hit the floor of the sitting room, was full of cans of beer. Henderson got glasses and poured out shots of the whisky, but the beer was drunk straight from the can, treated with the contumely which such watery brews merited. With a huge sighing effort Swacky gathered himself together like a runner preparing for the start of a marathon and commenced the longest speech of his life.

'What you've done here,' he said, 'you especially, Dave, and Alison, since we found those caves, is the best thing that's happened here ever. I mean, this place was dead, you know? A few sassenachs came here and a few toffs and a few of they White Settlers who bought crofties and turned them into holiday homes and came here for a few weeks a year and never went into the pubs and never got to know anyone local and never did anything for the Highlands except sort of look down on the local lads as layabouts an' boozers – not worth bothering with. But you an' Alison – an' Cal an' Rossie, too: he turned out all right in the end – you two made those caves into something, really brought the people in and put some life into the place, like, I mean everyone was getting something out of it where there wasn't any work before . . . What I mean to say is: what are we going to do about the Briggs mannie? See, I'm thinking you and Cal and the others are just going to let it all go . . . What I've been thinking all day since you told me about it is that if Simon took, for instance, a long walk in the hills and just sort of didn't come back . . . I mean it's happened often enough in the past and no-one's ever found them again . . . '

'Don't think we're not tempted, Swacky. People have been

dumped into bogs and fallen off crags and met their ends in all sorts of curious and horrible ways for a lot less, as you say, than we've all put into it. And I guess there's lots of ways of doing it that wouldn't arouse any suspicion. But could you live with yourself afterwards, ask yourself that?'

With no difficulty whatsoever, Swacky said, pouring another dram and downing it in a single practised movement. But Henderson knew his friend better at this moment than he knew himself. The fumes of alcohol were a fine suppressor of the social conscience but what might seem reasonable and even right in the moment of intoxication would revert to the utmost folly as bleak common sense came stealing in to replace its flights of fancy. And Swacky was already nodding and pulling himself awake again in a rapidly losing battle with unconsciousness. A short time later, after a few false starts at another speech, a few barely comprehensible murmurings, he slipped slowly sideways on the couch and sank into insensibility. Henderson looked down on him fondly, lifted up his feet and covered him with a blanket.

'Sleep sound, my lad, and wake without a hangover,' he said softly. 'In many ways you're the best of the lot of us.'

Swacky had played his best card; there were no cards left for the others to play, only Simon. It was him to deal.

It was not nearly so easy as one would have thought, Simon discovered during the following day, to unscramble a devious plot. Once a thing has gained the momentum of the Cnocdruidh Hill discoveries, uniting scholarship, money and public enthusiasm, the news media required rather more proof to expose the swindle than they ever required to establish it. For although he had telephoned a wide selection of local, provincial and national newspapers and the offices of the broadcast media, there were only two reporters at his hotel that morning. One was a lad just out of school who worked for the county's weekly newspaper, an idiosyncratic journal which still carried classified advertisements on its front page and occasionally issued from its leader page to its tiny readership of less than five thousand, solemn warnings to the Government and the nation and held

Britain up to task for failing to profit by similar warnings to change her ways issued in earlier weeks. The other reporter, who had stepped into Don Eglinton's shoes after he had been translated to London following his breaking of the original Cnocdruidh Caves story, was, as Eglinton had been, a 'stringer' for several national newspapers, but gave the impression that he had only attended Simon's press conference out of routine loyalty to his predecessor's success in this role. He said, quite audibly, 'Oh, my God,' and put away his notebook and little recorder when Simon prefaced his disclosures by an account of his conversion to born-again Christianity. He held up a hand, stopping Simon in mid-flow, and said: 'Excuse me, Mr . . . er . . . Higgins? But I was given to understand you had something to tell us about the Cnocdruidh Caves. Another reporter deals with religious affairs. Put it in the form of a letter to the editor. There's always room for that sort of thing there.' And he rose to go. The lad from the weekly, who was in awe of them both, was furiously making notes of what both of them had to say and clearly had no idea what it was about.

Simon protested: 'But I'm trying to explain why it is I have to speak out and denounce the Cnocdruidh Caves as a swindle. The Space God . . . the circles-and-lightning – everything in the caves was put there by local people, me included, so as to bring business into the area after the Loch Ness Monster fiasco – ' But the mention of Gods, circles and, in particular, the Loch Ness Monster, confirmed to the reporter, who was hardly listening, that Simon was merely another harmless religious crackpot of a type of which every newspaper in the land had more than enough.

'Mr Higgins,' the reporter said as he left, 'I'm sorry but I've got a lot of people to see today and I just haven't the time. I'm sorry – but ask yourself, Cnocdruidh Hill has been confirmed by some of the most respected scientists in the land, it's been front page news for half this year and thousands of people are going there every week. Is it likely that they're all wrong and you're right? Sorry, but I have to go.' And he went, leaving Simon in almost hysterical frustration, to unburden his soul to the apprentice who didn't know a neolithic quern from a cromlech and did not know how to spell either of them.

Simon was not so easily stopped, however. In fact, Simon, once he was on a crusade, was unstoppable. But he was dismayed and confused, so confused that he telephoned David Henderson, upon whom, over the years, he had grown to rely in moments of frustration and doubt, put his problem to him and asked for his help. There was a very long pause at the end of the line, then Henderson said: 'Do I understand you correctly, Simon? You're trying to get my help to blow the lid off the Cnocdruidh Project because you're finding it difficult to do it on your own?'

'Well, yes. I thought, maybe, after I'd explained how wrong we were to be doing it, you would have come round to my point of view – '

There was a strange sound at Henderson's end of the line and Simon took the receiver away from his ear, stared at it, shook it, and put it back to his ear again. 'Something wrong with the line – ' he began and then realised that what he was hearing from the other end was laughter. 'Hullo,' he said. 'Hullo. Hullo.'

When he could speak, Henderson said: 'Simon, I've already given you more help than I should. In fact, you'll never know how much. If it wasn't for me you might well be blowing bubbles in a peat bog at this very moment. So I'm afraid you're right out on your own, Simon, and I wish you the very worst of luck,' and the telephone went down.

Simon shook his head in wonder. He couldn't understand it, but even at the best of times, he thought, David Henderson had never struck him as a particularly stable character. Perhaps he was emotionally disturbed . . . He thought of speaking to Hugh Ross but on reflection abandoned the idea.

Over the next twenty-four hours Simon Briggs discovered that in a world which was used to lies and deceptions and accepted these things daily from presidents and prime ministers, from archbishops and from popes, it was a very difficult thing to tell the truth and to be believed: it seemed to be a commodity which was no longer recognised when it appeared, least of all by the news media. Simon, however, was indefatigable and the snubs he received from the news media merely strengthened his determnation to be heard.

It is entirely likely that Simon would never have found an audience for his disclosure if it had not been for a singular stroke of ill-fortune for the Ross-Jefferson-Henderson axis which was a stroke of the utmost luck for Simon's purposes. Quietly and diligently Dr Nathaniel Mould, his chief assistant Martin Ryle and several other postgraduate students who were eager for material for their doctorate theses, were working away with scraper, brush and sieve in the inner cave, carefully picking, layer by microscopic layer at the earth around and beneath the spot where they had unearthed the astonishing gold plaque. The work went on in relays, almost round the clock, often with the throngs of visitors who hourly crowded the platforms peering down at the painstaking meticulous workers who, for the most part, ignored them and their well-intentioned advice.

It was Dr Mould's hope – a hope with which he had fired his eager team – that there might be another plaque, or at least another segment of the one which he had discovered, lying in the earth close by or directly underneath the first discovery and the search was therefore very slow and very detailed and the earth was being removed almost, it would seem, at one molecule at a time. But such is the nature of an archaeological dig that, slow and detailed though the work was, excitement throbbed in the air.

Dr Mould was there himself when, towards the end of that day there was a hiss of excitement from one of his young workers which brought him scurrying over and down on his hands and knees. With the end of a wooden spatula the student had uncovered the edge, the straight edge and a corner of something which was most definitely not a part of the natural stony floor and which seemed to be made of a corroded metal.

Dr Mould shoved him out of the way and, for the next five hours, with only his trusted amanuensis Ryle for co-worker, scraped and brushed, poked, eased and blew the dust of aeons from the object. None of the other workers left the scene, jammed shoulder to shoulder, oblivious of thirst or hunger or cramp.

David Henderson heard of the excitement during the afternoon and, in amazement and puzzlement, went up to the site with Cal. The nearest they were allowed to it was a few yards away and they were confined to the tourist platform. During a movement of the close-packed students below them they at last caught a glimpse of the artifact Dr Mould was with such care retrieving from its dusty lair. 'Oh, Christ!' Henderson said, and he and Cal left the spot and walked down the hill, arms around each other's shoulders, without deviation straight to Cal's Manager's bar, where he took down a very rare old whisky, one of the few which still was sealed with a cork, withdrew the cork with care, threw it away, and poured two generous measures and sat down to finish it.

The work in the inner cave went on. Perhaps there was a stage at which, if it had only been himself and Ryle at work instead of a team of eight, Dr Mould might have been tempted to keep his discovery a secret. But the time when this could have been done was long past. Now the outlines of the buried object had taken full shape. The gleam of metal was unmistakable and the shape too; it was an undoubted rectangle about eight inches long by five inches wide, and, as they lifted it out of its socket in the earth, it proved to be about an inch and a half deep. Held by forceps and tweezers it was lifted up with tremulous care and placed on a tray. One of the students adjusted the fierce glare of the overhead lights so that it could be seen naked and shadowless in the brilliant glare. He took a photograph.

It was an ingot. No, it was a box. It was a box with a lid. Forceps and tweezers raised the lid. It came off with a little difficulty and was laid to one side. There were objects inside the box. One by one they were lifted out and laid in a row on the tray alongside the box.

One of the objects was a pencil, a lead pencil. It was dusty, but in gold lettering along the length of it could be discerned the words, in English, Reeves, H.B. 3. Another of the objects was a very battered briar pipe. A third object was an empty white packet with an inner envelope of silver foil. And, on the uppermost side was a red circle imprinted with the legend, Lucky Strike. And, lower down, the words: It's Toasted! There was a penknife with two broken blades. There was a very hard lump of something which looked like ancient chewing gum, well-chewed and discarded. There was a 1932 copper penny with the head of George V on it. There was a piece of string.

One by one the archaeologists slowly left the scene and went home. Dr Mould was the last to leave and he switched off the lights, took a last long look around and tramped up to the surface. He left everything below ground exactly as it was. When he reached the perimeter fence, watched by MacGillivray, he locked the gate. And then he looked at the key in his hand. Suddenly he whirled around and threw it as far down the hill as he could and then he plodded off in the gloaming while MacGillivray stared after him, a hand to his head.

Henderson said to Cal as they sat, one on each side of a little table opposite to each other, an empty bottle and two empty glasses between them, chins propped on their elbows, looking into each other's eyes: 'It was the plaque that was the mistake. If he hadn't found old Andrew's treasure underneath it he would have made some sort of explanation for finding it down there – some kids had strayed down there years ago. Something like that. We shoulda left well enough alone. 'Salways a mistake, wouldn' you say, Cal, to gild the bloody lily?'

'Hell,' said Cal. 'He's just a drag-ass dude. Don't you pay any never no mind to him, pal.'

And after this, of course, Simon Briggs had no difficulty at all in getting the news media to listen to his confessions. Henderson, Cal, the Squadron Leader, and even Swacky when they tracked him down, gave them a snooty 'no comment'. Dr Nathaniel Mould could not be found at all.

You poor old darling,

I might be with you ere you get this. I'm flying up immediately and will telephone you from Inverness. There's nothing to keep me away now, is there? Is there?

Love, Ally.

She arrived on the day the newspapers carried Simon's confession. NORTHERN HOTELIER CLAIMS PAINTED CAVES A FAKE, said one. ARCHAEOLOGICAL SENSATION WAS ONLY SCOTCH MIST, said another. GREATEST ARCHAEOLOGY SWINDLE OF THE CENTURY – HOW WE DID IT, said a third.

Alison said: 'David, stop avoiding my eye and twitching about. Do you want me to come and live with you, or not?'

'Of course I do. But I'm too old.'

'Too old implies: too old – for what? You're not too old for me. Am I too young for you?'

'No, of course not. But, at the risk of sounding all Mills and Boon, you're Spring and Summer, Ally. I'm old grey Autumn.'

She hugged him. She said: 'Most of the best things don't ripen till the Autumn. We'll have an Indian Summer.'

She kissed him. They kissed.

The three of them, Henderson, Alison and Swacky, stood on the very summit of Cnocdruidh Hill. In all the time he had lived there, Henderson realised, it was the first time he had ever climbed all the way to the top. Below them, in a landscape which was beginning already to take on some of the russet hues of autumn, now quite small and unimportant, lay those things which had obsessed them with such fierce hopes and despairs, such rages and laughter, shrunk now to a temporary insignificance: a toy tea-room with dinky cars and buses drawn up around it: a miniature cave entrance with doll's house steps leading down to it and around it a play-farm fence. And over there, a foot or two away, in a pygmy bend of the river, the Lilliputian roofs and car parks of Cal's Cnocdruidh Lodge.

And invisible at this distance, but undoubtedly somewhere there, the small figure of Dr Nathaniel Mould contemplating with rage the sneers of his academic colleagues and the ruination of his career.

'Don't you feel sorry for him at all?' Henderson said.

'No,' said Alison. 'And it's time I told you why. It's only a little story, and a very common one. It happens all the time. And it's too beautiful a day to waste time on it so I'll make it the shortest story you ever heard, or nearly. It was about three years ago and we were excavating a site in Glasgow where a number of nineteenth-century tenements had been demolished and before the bulldozers moved in to excavate the foundations for yet another of those office-block-supermarket developments. I was one of Dr Mould's postgraduate students, working at subsistence wages while I gathered material for my doctorate thesis. We were turning up quite a lot of stuff, interesting enough in its way, of medieval hearths, hutments and pottery. It had been going on for weeks with the doctor holding a watching brief while we scraped and classified and labelled. It was becoming routine, and he wasn't there very much: just a quick visit and a conference session every now and then to make sure we were proceeding on the right lines.

'And then I stumbled on something quite exciting. For a week I had it to myself. The others just congratulated me, patted me on the back and left me to it. It was the sort of thing they'd all dreamed about themselves, but there is a generosity and morality amongst most of us – a lot of help and support which is given to the lucky ones when something like this happens and really no jealousy at all. You see, by some sort of anomaly in the strata of the site, I came across a perfect little Bronze Age smithy, with a positive mine of axe heads, broken knives, furnace, ingots – one of the most significant discoveries of its kind ever made. I only stopped working at it for a few hours a day to get some sleep, and then I'd be back again, digging, classifying, photographing – all the usual things.

'Well, at the weekend Dr Mould arrived. To say he was excited is the meiosis of all time. He was beside himself. And he was kindness and helpfulness itself. He re-arranged and re-classified my notes for me and took them into safe keeping when the dig was over and we had to return to our various places. I was attached to a museum at the time in the south.

'Well, you can read all about it, if you're interested, in the journals of the British Archaeological Society – a series of neat little essays by Dr Nathaniel Mould on Bronze Age encampments in northern Britain . . . '

'You mean he pinched it?'

'The lot. It was published and I was pre-empted before I knew what was happening. A short while later he got his present Chair – and I never got my doctorate . . . '

Henderson wondered how Alison could talk so calmly, so without bitterness. There was a long pause as they gazed down at the miniature sunlit landscape below.

Swacky spoke. He said: 'That Dr Mould: is he a real professor, then?'

Henderson nodded.

Swacky said: '"A" levels and College, an' all that stuff?'

Henderson nodded again.

There was another little pause during which they observed a long line of sheep, like soiled pearls on a string, far down the valley, being herded slowly in single file towards the farm, their cries of distress reaching very faintly to the top of the hill.

'Well, I'll tell you,' said Swacky, who had never had much of an opinion of Dr Mould's intelligence, still looking down at the distant sheep, 'he may be bloody well educated, an' that, but there's far wiser eating grass.'

CHAPTER SIXTEEN

Winter had been, scoured the hills and valleys white and left in flurries of hail and cold rain. Easter is not a religious festival in most of presbyterian Scotland but it is still the time when, like the migrating greylag geese, the first tourists arrive in the Highlands from the south. Among the tourist-orientated fraternity there is always at this time an air of educated prophecy, a casting of the bones and reading of the omens in an attempt to make an assessment of the tourist trade for the whole coming season, based on the volume and character of this first trickle.

Everyone in the Achnairn, Laidmore and Kincardine area awaited, therefore, their first Easter influx with the most anxious trepidation. After the furious controversies which had featured for many weeks in the popular national newspapers, in more serious weeklies and magazines and in erudite journals, on the great archaeological confidence trick perpetrated at Cnocdruidh Hill, would any visitors come at all?

Cal Jefferson was back from his annual Inland Revenue Service tax-flight to the United States and he seemed to be brimming over with enthusiasm. He said: 'Hell, those turkeys will be back, Dave, don't you worry. These jive-ass reporters are playing into our hands; you know as well as me, it doesn't matter what they're saying as long as they're saying something.' But his bars and buses were shining, polished and empty. 'See what I've been doing while I've been away,' he said, and, taking Henderson by the arm, led him into one of his store-rooms. He switched on the light and there was the gleam of gold – or something that looked like gold – in heaps and windrows on the floors, on shelves and tables. Henderson looked closer, picked up some of the objects. They were all in the curious shape of the Cnocdruidh Caves plaque and inscribed with exact miniatures of the same symbols. There were straightforward copies of the plaque itself, but there were also earrings, pendants, bracelets and key rings. 'Christ!' he said. 'You don't do things by halves, do you Cal?'

Cal said: 'All genuine pinchbeck, all authentic Highland souvenirs. Had them made by a little workshop in Taiwan while I was away.'

'Bit of a problem to get rid of if the tourists don't come, though, Cal?'

'Hell, they'll come.' He sounded confident. Henderson started to chuckle. He said: 'Come along with me to the pottery and I'll show you what Ally and I have been doing during the winter.'

And there on the display shelves of his walkaround pottery were hundreds of ashtrays, plates and vases with not only the Cnocdruidh plaque motif, but also the linked circles and lightning, the pantheon of mythological beasts from the first cave and the winged and helmeted figure of the Space God.

'So, who's the optimist now?' said Cal. 'And what's the Wing Commander been up to?'

Squadron Leader Ross had spent the winter buttoned up tight in his winter quarters, with the big house closed down while he and his wife saw the cold weather out, as was their practice, in the small cosy gatehouse of the little estate. He had made no plans until he could see what the spring would bring.

Of them all, Simon Briggs was quite unperturbed and conscience-clear, having turned his establishment into a temperance hotel – a sublime anomaly in a hard-drinking region — and having, as a consequence, become once more firmly under the dominance of his bank manager.

One other change there had been and that was largely an

administrative one. The Kincardine Cabal, no longer forced into secrecy, had come to the surface as the Cnocdruidh Hill Promotion Committee with a chairman, a treasurer and parliamentary rules of debate. The archaeological establishment being no longer interested in the Caves, the committee had acquired the site from Monty Dickinson who, now having sold the same property twice, only wanted to be disassociated from the whole ungentlemanly business. Plans for their development were only waiting the turn of events.

'I'll give you a quote to cheer you up,' Alison said one day as they waited to see what was going to happen. 'I found it the other day, and it's from the great Marquis of Montrose, who tramped all over these hills fighting for both sides, Covenanters and the King, and lost his last battle not too many miles from here. He was a great gambler. He wrote, when he was a student at St Andrew's:

'He either fears his fate too much
Or his deserts are small
That dares not put it to the touch
To win or lose it all.'

And a few days later, Daniel Beardsley arrived, like Moses, out of the southern desert, at the head of a small army of his zealots, in campers, caravans and tents, and was made welcome in the Cnocdruidh Hill Promotion Committee's caravan park. Daniel had lost not one jot or tittle of his faith, and indeed the attempt to discredit the authenticity of the Caves was entirely what he and his followers had expected. It renewed their faith and was clearly just a part of the usual conspiracy sustained by State and bureaucracy to hide the truth and perpetuate belief in the standard, safe, outworn dogma of Christendom. He held a revival meeting on the hillside, addressing a large crowd through a megaphone.

'All down the ages,' he shouted, 'governments and communities have tried to use the beliefs of the people to bolster their own power. And if they can't institutionalise a belief, then they set out to destroy it. In the old days they made martyrs of them, tortured them and burnt them at the stake. Today the methods are different, but the purpose is the same – to keep the strings of religion in the politicians' hands so that they can manipulate you all. And so they attempt to destroy the incontrovertible evidence of the Cnocdruidh Caves and the Cnocdruidh symbols which point so clearly to an authority which is far beyond that of ordinary men and governments – a message from beyond the stars. One day they will be confounded, and we hope soon, when those visitors, so vastly far beyond us in science and intellect, come back again in glory to see if their message left to us here, has been understood.

'And now I want you all to be absolutely silent for a minute while we send our thoughts upwards and outwards to those who dwell beyond our universe and beseech them to return.'

The silence which followed was so profound that only the sibilance of the wind in the grasses, the far-off calling of the new lambs and the beating of leaf on leaf could be heard. No amount of noise, no amount of cheering and chanting could have displayed half so clearly the faith of his followers in the prophet Daniel.

The first trickle, then, grew into a flood and the flood grew until there was no room to hold all the people who had come, either to see what they knew to be a fraud, or because they neither knew nor cared whether it was genuine or not. There was no stopping them.

And, now that they had control over them, Swacky was all for adding further paintings to those already in the Cnocdruidh Caves. 'Hell, boys,' he said to Mr and Mrs David Henderson, 'I don't know what you think you was doing all the autumn down in that caves but you could have got some right artists in there and some real bright paint instead of that foosty stuff you put on it. It's not too late now – I know a couple of decorator-mannies what'll be glad to do a homer an' cover the whole thing for you in real, you know . . . er . . . Friesians – '

'Friezes – frescoes, Swacky?'

'Aye. That things. No? Well, just let me know if you change your minds. I'll get you a damn good price.'